W9-BHZ-781

"YOU WEAR MY RING, LADY DEIRDRE"

"It is in my jewel box at home. This engagement is a farce, my lord, and I insist you treat me entirely as a stranger."

"Oh, I think not." He trapped her head with a hand curled around her neck and seared her with a slanting kiss.

Deirdre scrubbed at her mouth. "How dare you, sir!"

"Don't be foolish. I dare a great deal more than that, but I'm unlikely to go much further without encouragement."

"Which you will never receive," she said hotly. "I give you fair warning, Lord Everdon. Do that again and I'll slap your face!"

Praise for Jo Beverley

"One of the best
historical romance authors now writing."
Mary Balogh

"Regency superstar
Jo Beverley bedazzles . . .
with an enchanting masterpiece . . .
that is sheer romantic perfection . . .
outrageously delightful . . .
pure storytelling genius."
Melinda Helfer, *Romantic Times*

Other Regency Romances by
Jo Beverley

EMILY AND THE DARK ANGEL
THE FORTUNE HUNTER
THE STANFORTH SECRETS

Other **Regency Romances**
from Avon Books

CLARISSA *by Cathleen Clare*
FAIR SCHEMER *by Sally Martin*
THE MISCHIEVOUS MAID *by Rebecca Robbins*
THE MUCH MALIGNED LORD *by Barbara Reeves*
THE UNMATCHABLE MISS MIRABELLA *by Gillian Grey*

Coming Soon

TOURNAMENT OF HEARTS *by Cathleen Clare*

Avon Books are available at special quantity discounts for bulk purchases for sales promotions, premiums, fund raising or educational use. Special books, or book excerpts, can also be created to fit specific needs.

For details write or telephone the office of the Director of Special Markets, Avon Books, Dept. FP, 1350 Avenue of the Americas, New York, New York 10019, 1-800-238-0658.

Deirdre and Don Juan

JO BEVERLEY

AVON BOOKS ◆ NEW YORK

If you purchased this book without a cover, you should be aware that
this book is stolen property. It was reported as "unsold and destroyed"
to the publisher, and neither the author nor the publisher has received
any payment for this "stripped book."

DEIRDRE AND DON JUAN is a original publication of Avon Books.
This work has never before appeared in book form. This work is a novel.
Any similarity to actual persons or events is purely coincidental.

AVON BOOKS
A division of
The Hearst Corporation
1350 Avenue of the Americas
New York, New York 10019

Copyright © 1993 by Jo Beverley
Published by arrangement with the author
Library of Congress Catalog Card Number: 93-90402
ISBN: 0-380-77281-7

All rights reserved, which includes the right to reproduce this book or
portions thereof in any form whatsoever except as provided by the U. S.
Copyright Law. For information address Alice Orr Literary Agency,
305 Madison Avenue, Suite 1166, New York, New York 10165.

First Avon Books Printing: December 1993

AVON TRADEMARK REG. U.S. PAT. OFF. AND IN OTHER COUNTRIES, MARCA
REGISTRADA, HECHO EN U.S.A.

Printed in the U.S.A.

RA   10 9 8 7 6 5 4 3 2 1

1

The news of his wife's death caught the Earl of Everdon in his mistress's bed. He knew most of the world would consider this unremarkable for a man generally known as Don Juan, but he could only see it as a social solecism. Even as he read the disturbing letter, he directed a few choice epithets toward his thick-skulled secretary. What had possessed young Morrow to send it here?

After all, he'd not clapped eyes on his wife for close to ten years, so this travel-stained record of Genie's demise could surely have waited until he returned home.

Noblesse obliged, however, and he detached himself from Barbara Vayne's demanding fingers, swung out of bed, and began to pull on his clothes.

He was a tall, handsome man of thirty, who had inherited a distinctly Latin cast to his features from his Spanish mother. His skin had a yearlong darkness unusual in England; his eyes were a deep velvet brown under smooth, heavy lids; his brows and lashes were richly dark. His hair, however, had been touched by his English heritage, and showed sherry gold lights in the afternoon sun. This merely served to emphasize the darker cast of his skin.

"Don, what's the matter?" his abandoned lover demanded plaintively, pouting her lush lips.

He fastened his pantaloons. "A family crisis."

Barbara threw off the covers and arched. "Something more important than this?"

He tried never to be unkind to a woman, so he paid her the homage of a hot, regretful look, but didn't halt his dressing. His mind was on other things.

There were disturbing aspects to this situation.

Ten years of freedom were over.

He had married Iphegenia Brandon when only twenty, and just down from Cambridge. In retrospect, it had not been wise, and the subsequent disasters had been excruciatingly embarrassing, but he had grown accustomed. In time, he had even discovered that there were advantages to being an abandoned husband.

For the past ten years the Matchmaking Mamas had regretfully ignored him. He had been able to behave with remarkable rashness without any possibility of being forced to the altar. His only brother's death the year before had caused him to investigate the possibility of divorce, but he had intended to select a bride with great care well before he was known to be available.

Now, however, he was fair prey in the martrimonial hunt. Absurd though it was, once this news broke, even someone like Barbara—the wanton widow of a highly disreputable infantry captain—might think she had a chance of getting Lord Everdon to the altar.

He didn't neglect the courtesy of a heated farewell kiss, but he first imprisoned Barbara's hands above her head, just to be sure he escaped her bedroom safely.

Then Mark Juan Carlos Renfrew, Earl of Everdon and lord of a score of minor properties, walked through the streets of Mayfair feeling vulnerable for the first time in his adult life.

* * *

During the walk his wariness turned to irritation, and the irritation found a focus. When he arrived at his Marlborough Square mansion, he stalked into his secretary's study and tossed the letter on David Morrow's desk. "Preaching, I'll abide, but not outright malice. You are dismissed."

The young man was already on his feet. Now he wavered, sheet white. "I'm *what* . . .?"

"You heard me. I will give you an adequate reference as to the conscientiousness of your work."

"But . . . but *why*, my lord?"

Everdon was arrested. Young Morrow was nothing if not honest, and his bewilderment rang true. "Why did you send that letter over to Barbara's house?"

"But . . . but your wife, my lord. She's *dead!*"

"Six months ago, according to that Greek priest."

"But even so . . . you would want to know . . . You wouldn't want, at such a moment . . ." The young man flushed red with embarrassment.

Everdon swore with exasperation. "David, my beloved Genie ran off with an Italian diplomat nearly ten years ago, within six months of our ill-judged and juvenile marriage. She has since worked her way through the best—or worst—part of the European nobility. Why the devil should I care that she's finally met her end?"

But Everdon did care, and knew his untypical foul mood was a direct consequence of that distant death.

Young Morrow's lips quivered slightly, but he stiffened his spine. "I am sorry for so misjudging the situation, my lord. I will just collect my possessions—"

"Stubble it," said Everdon curtly, fairness reasserting itself. As the fourth son of an impoverished family, David Morrow had his way to make in the world, and he was an excellent employee. It wasn't the lad's fault that he was as prissy as a cloistered nun. It amused Everdon to surround himself with righteousness.

"I apologize for misjudging you." Everdon smiled, deliberately using his charm to soothe. "Sit down and get on with your work, David. But if you're researching that matter of the relief of debtors for me, remember my interest as always is pragmatic, not moral or sanctimonious. Give me facts and figures, not sermons."

The secretary sat with a thump, relief flooding his round face. "Thank you, my lord. Of course, my lord . . ."

Everdon waved away gratitude. "As you see, I am decidedly out of curl."

"Er . . . because of your wife, my lord?"

Everdon's smile became twisted. "You could put it that way. I'm out of curl because I'm going to have to choose my next wife in a devil of a hurry."

Upon leaving his secretary, Everdon went straight to his mother's suite.

Lucetta, Dowager Countess of Everdon, was a handsome woman whose strong-boned face clearly showed her Spanish heritage. Though she was fifty, her black hair held no touch of gray, and her fine dark eyes could still flash with emotion. She was, however, afflicted with a hip disease that made even walking painful, and she largely kept to her rooms, receiving guests and engaging in her passion—embroidery. Everdon kissed her cheek, then surveyed her latest piece, an exquisite working of purple pansies on gossamer silk.

"That is very beautiful, Mother, but I can hardly see it as a chairback." He spoke Spanish, as he always did when alone with his mother.

She chuckled. "Assuredly not, my dear. In truth, I am not sure what I shall do with it. Lady Deirdre has infected me with this notion of needlework for its own sake. I suppose if nothing else occurs, it will make a panel for a gown."

He shook his head. "The lady does not exist who is worthy of such ornamentation."

"What nonsense you speak, Marco. It is just embroidery. Poor women do work as fine for pennies to ornament our society blossoms."

"I disagree." He studied the work in her frame. "That is a special piece. It's the difference between a portrait by Lawrence, and one by an itinerant artist. Lady Deirdre has a case to make. When it is finished, I shall have that work framed."

Lucetta studied her son, her only child now his younger brother was dead, killed at Vittoria. She sensed an unusual uneasiness in him. "What brings you here today, Marco?"

He glanced up, and his long-lashed dark eyes reminded her poignantly of her brother at the same age, and in a scrape. She knew she really shouldn't blame Marco for his philandering when he had inherited her family's devastating charms, but she did. Or at least, she worried.

He evaded her question. "Do I need an excuse to visit you, *Madrecita?*"

"Of course not, but it is rare to see you in the afternoon. There are so many competing attractions."

A faint color rose in his cheeks. Beneath the olive skin many would not have noticed it, but she was accustomed to reading such things. "Well?" she demanded.

He looked down at a glossy boot. "Genie's dead."

Lucetta's needle paused for a moment. "At last," she said.

"Mother!"

She continued setting stitches. "Am I supposed to feign grief? I am not sorry. I am not surprised. I can even guess the cause of her death."

"Mother, really . . ."

"You English are so mealy-mouthed. She was a wretched young woman, and doubtless died miserably of the pox. Her suffering may save her immortal soul."

"Hardly the sentiment of a good English Protestant," he pointed out.

"I became a Protestant for your father. I reverted to the true faith when he died, as you know." She fixed him with a direct look. "This is good. Now you can marry again."

"That is my duty," he said bleakly.

Lucetta's face softened. "Not all women are as Iphegenia was, dearest one. And you are much wiser now." She sighed. "I have blamed myself most deeply."

He moved restlessly to a window overlooking the extensive gardens of his mansion. "It wasn't your fault, love. I was mad for her."

"But you were young, Marco. Not yet twenty. It was my duty as your mother to be wise for you."

Lucetta abandoned her work before she made a botch of it. It was time for truth. "I saw your grandfather and uncles in you, you see. Women came to them so easily, they could not resist. It caused great problems. Genie was so beautiful, so passionate. When you loved her, I thought she might satisfy you and keep you safe."

He turned to face her. "And instead, I failed to satisfy her."

"No man could satisfy her. She proved that over and again."

He said nothing—he never had on this subject— but she read old anguish in his face. "Do you still feel tenderly toward her, Marco?"

He turned again, hiding from her. "Feel for her? I can hardly remember her. I remember how I felt . . ." His voice turned brisk. "Never fear. I know I must marry. With Richard gone, and Cousin Ian ailing, I have no choice. I can hardly leave the earldom to

Kevin, fond though I am of him. I must get an heir. It is merely a matter of finding the right woman."

"That should not be difficult. You will be the prize of the Marriage Mart." Lucetta saw him wince and struggled to keep a straight face. As she took up her needle again, she thought that the next weeks could be amusing. She was determined, however, that this time her son would make a good marriage. He probably wouldn't believe it, but he was capable of making the right woman a wonderful husband.

"I suppose I shall have to see what is still available this late in the Season," he said. "At least I'm not looking for a Belle or an heiress. Just someone quiet, plain, and content to stay at home."

Lucetta's needle froze. "Quiet? Plain? That is hardly to your taste."

"It is in wives," he said crisply. "I am hoping you have a candidate in mind."

"I will have nothing to do with such foolishness," she stated. "You will join the social whirl and find someone who appeals to you."

"I am recently bereaved," he said piously.

His mother spat a Spanish opinion of that excuse. "Six months bereaved."

Everdon leaned against a wall, arms folded. "Very well, the truth. It's too dangerous out there. I intend to be in control of this selection."

"Foolish boy. Are you afraid of the Matchmaking Mamas?"

His grin was disarming. "Terrified. I've worn the armor of my marriage for so long, I feel naked without it." He put on a most beguiling smile. "If you love me, *mama mia*, you will find me a safe candidate. You can't persuade me you don't know every one of this year's crop."

Lucetta placed a careful stitch. "Maud Tiverton, then."

"Maud Tiverton! She looks like a cross between Torquemada and a pug."

Lucetta smiled sweetly at him. "At least you could be sure no man would steal her from under your nose."

This time anyone would have seen the color in his cheeks. He made no defense or denial.

"Oh, my dear," said Lucetta seriously. "This is no way to choose your companion in life. Give it time."

He shook his head. "Life can be chancy—look at Richard and Ian. I know my duty." He twisted his gold signet ring. "Since Ian fell sick and recovery became unlikely, I'd even made moves to obtain a divorce, though I hate the thought of a public airing of Genie's behavior. I know the distress it would cause her parents . . ."

"At least that is no longer necessary," said Lucetta gently.

"True. And I'd be a fool to waste the last weeks of the Season. What better time to find a bride? If you won't help, I will just have to pick one blindfolded." He shrugged. "Marriage is a mere lottery anyway. If one doesn't spend too long anguishing over the ticket, there's less pain if it turns out a loser."

Lucetta rested her hands on her frame and considered him with a frown. She could tell he was in earnest and would do this foolish thing. "Very well, then. If that is how it is, I think you should marry Deirdre."

"Deirdre Stowe?" he said blankly.

"Lady Deirdre Stowe, daughter of the Earl of Harby. My young friend, whom you have met here now and again. That Deirdre."

"Why?"

"Why not?" she asked briskly. "Is not one lottery ticket as good as another? She is wellborn and wellbred. Her portion is comfortable. She is composed, but not weak. She will be well able to run your households and raise your children. It does, however, seem highly unlikely that some man will try to filch her from you—men being shortsighted in these matters—and even less likely that she would dream of being filched. Furthermore," she added tartly, "I have more concern for my comfort than you have for yours, and I like her."

He shrugged. "The best argument of all. Consider it done."

Her eyes flashed angrily. "Does it not occur to you, you wretch, that she might refuse you?"

He quirked a brow. "No. Will she?"

She glared at him but then sighed and shook her head. "It is unlikely, I fear. It would do you good to be refused for once. One reason I suggested Deirdre—and I am beginning to regret it—is that she is having a miserable time. She doesn't speak of it, but I am sure she is a wallflower."

"Men probably just don't notice her," Everdon pointed out. "She's so thin and wishy-washy, I hardly notice her when she's here in the room." He looked around, in the pretense that the young lady might in fact be present.

Lucetta shook her head. "It will not do, will it? I will try to think of someone more suitable."

"Nonsense. She is ideal. I believe the Ashbys are holding a soirée tonight. Will she be there?"

"It is likely. Her mother drags her everywhere, firmly convinced that one day a miracle will happen, and Deirdre will turn into a Toast before everyone's eyes."

He grinned. "And so she will. She is about to sweep Don Juan off his feet."

Lucetta focused on him the full force of a maternal look. "Marco, I warn you, hurt Deirdre and you will pray for the fires of hell."

That evening Lord Everdon commanded his valet to produce his dark evening clothes and kid slippers, a sure sign that he was intent on Polite Society and not debauchery. Joseph Bing's conscience could for once be at ease as he used his considerable skills to turn his employer out to perfection.

Joseph's conscience had frequently been troubled since he had been saved and become a follower of John Wesley.

He told his friends at the Chapel that he only kept his post with the earl because his employer indulgently allowed him plenty of free time to attend to Chapel business, and the whole of Sunday off. The truth was that he was very fond of Everdon, whom he'd served since his Cambridge days. He found professional satisfaction in valeting such a fine figure of a man, and he hoped to save him from perdition.

The perils Joseph feared were twofold. On the one hand, the earl was clearly given over to fornication of the most blatant kind. That placed him in risk of damnation. The far greater danger, however, was that he would have a sudden religious experience and follow his mother into the maw of papacy.

Joseph Bing was determined to prevent that fate, and to somehow wean the earl from his fondness for loose women. He could hardly hope Everdon would ever join the Wesleyan fraternity, but a virtuous lifestyle and a sober adherence to the Church of England would make Joseph a very happy man.

As Joseph finished shaving his master's smooth, brown skin, the earl said, "Has the news somehow escaped, Joseph? I am a widower. You may felicitate me."

Joseph gave thanks he had put down the razor before that disconcerting announcement. "Congratulations, my lord," he said, though it hardly seemed proper. He remembered sadly the beautiful, willful Iphegenia, and the brief fury of youthful passion that had been that ill-fated marriage. In the aftermath he had feared for the young earl's sanity. It was a miracle really that it had merely turned him to vice ...

"You needn't sound so squeamish," said Everdon as he stood and shrugged off the cloth that protected his shirt. "Genie died six months ago." He deftly tied a cravat, then allowed Joseph to ease on his brocade waistcoat and plain, elegant jacket. "I merely forewarn you of possible changes. I intend to marry again."

"That is good news, milord," said Joseph as he smoothed the cloth over broad shoulders. His joy was honest. That's what the earl needed—the love of a good woman.

But would he choose one?

"I'm glad you think so. Time will tell." Everdon surveyed himself in the mirror. "The pearl, I think." When the valet brought the pearl pin, Everdon said, "And how are matters at the Chapel?"

Joseph had thought at one time that his master mocked him when he said such things, but it appeared not to be the case. "Very well, thank you, milord. Your support for our school is much appreciated."

Everdon deftly adjusted his cravat and fixed the pin. "Have you ever thought of providing a refuge for unfortunate women?"

Joseph glanced at his employer. What lay behind this? He cleared his throat. "You would perhaps mean streetwalkers, my lord?"

"And others too unsavory to be helped by the tight-lipped brigade. There must be many women who make unfortunate choices and come to regret them. What becomes of them?"

Joseph foresaw trouble with some of the Chapel members, but he was a true seeker after good. "I believe our Savior would want us to help such women, as He helped Mary Magdalene."

"So do I. I will be most generous in my support of

such a project." Everdon swung on his cloak. "I dislike seeing any woman in distress."

It was said in his usual flippant manner, but Joseph detected some deeper meaning behind it. Did Lord Everdon have a particular woman in mind? Well, if housing one of the earl's old loves was the price of helping hundreds, it was a small price to pay.

Everdon took his hat and gloves from Joseph. "The news of my widowing is not to be made public just yet, Joseph. I prefer not to create a stir. To be more precise," he added with a flickering smile, "I do not want to alert the hunt. Now I go to pick a lottery ticket. Wish me luck, but don't wait up."

As Joseph tidied the room, he muttered, "The nonsense he do talk. Now, why would he want a lottery ticket, rich as he is?"

The Ashby soirée was being hosted by Lord and Lady Randal Ashby, dashing leaders of Society, in the mansion of Lord Randal's father, the Duke of Tyne. Everdon had learned from his invitation that it was in honor of Randal's cousin, Harry Crisp, and his promised bride, Miss Amy de Lacy. He knew Harry slightly, but not the girl; he was not in the habit of attending the more formal social affairs.

The event was well under way when Everdon arrived, and he had to search out his host and hostess.

"Lord Everdon, we're honored," said Sophie Ashby, affecting satirical amazement, but she smiled warmly as he kissed her hand. They were well acquainted, for Randal did not hesitate to bring his wife to more racy entertainments.

She was a vivacious young woman with something of a gamine appearance, but a sweetly curved figure. Everdon had a taste for curves in his women. He thought of thin Deirdre Stowe, and suffered a pang of doubt.

He gave Sophie a genuinely admiring smile. "I thought I'd see how the polite world went along."

"Being more familiar with the impolite?" she queried with a twinkle of humor.

He laughed. He also admired a woman who could bandy words. "They christened me Don Juan in my school days, and my fate was sealed."

Lord Randal remarked, "I earned the nickname of the Bright Angel. I managed to outgrow it, Don."

"Did you indeed? Yet I detect a glitter still, and the touch of the wicked that was behind the name."

"How true," said Sophie with a teasing look at her handsome, blond husband. Randal's response was a glance of heated yet discreet intimacy.

Everdon realized with a pang that he'd shared something similar once with Genie, who hadn't really loved him, and was dead . . .

"So," Randal was asking, "why are you here, Don? I assure you, this evening ain't about to become exciting. All the ancient family connections are here, for a start."

"I merely thought to see how the *ton* is enduring the dying days of this summer of excitement."

"We cannot always have visiting kings and emperors to amuse us," Sophie pointed out.

"I'd have thought everyone would be relieved to have a little peace and quiet after endless parades and displays."

"Do I detect a jaded tone?" asked Lord Randal. "You have to confess, Don, it was a livelier Season than we've seen in years. And as a bonus, we are now permitted to dance the waltz without censure."

Everdon grinned. "That doubtless takes all the thrill out of it."

"I fear you are right," said Sophie, "though I have a marked partiality for the dance, wicked or no. And you," she said to Everdon, "are very skilled at it."

"That," pointed out her husband, "if you didn't recognize it, was a hint."

"I'm positively bruised by the force of it. Do I gather you won't dance with your wife, Randal?"

"Of course he will," said Sophie, "but as hosts, we have to attend to the needs of our guests. We are to have three waltzes, and he can't dance every one with me."

Everdon kissed her hand and held it to his heart. "If you were mine, enchanting one, I would dance every waltz with you, host or no."

Sophie gurgled with laughter. "Are you trying to seduce me under Randal's very nose?"

Everdon smiled into her eyes. "Only if you are willing, *querida*."

Sophie looked rather startled. "But you never entangle yourself with happily married women."

"Perhaps I am just more discreet with them ..."

Randal removed his wife from Everdon's grasp. "How is it no one has shot you, Don?"

Everdon took time for a pinch of snuff. "Perhaps because I'm a crack shot, old boy."

Randal smiled, but there was an edge on it. "I'm better."

Everdon laughed and dropped his pose. "Don't raise your hackles. I'm a charitable foundation, don't you know? I only interest myself with unhappy women, and Sophie appears to be entirely happy, alas."

"Yes, I am," said Sophie with a playful flutter of her fan. "What a shame ..."

Her husband groaned. "I'm sure there are a great number of unhappy women in this room, Sophie. Why not steer the charitable foundation in their direction."

Sophie looked at Everdon. "Well, my lord?"

He bowed, hand on heart. " 'Tis my very purpose in coming. I am corrupted by my mother's Romish beliefs and fear for my immortal soul. I am here to do reparation for my many sins. Lead me to the most deserving cases!"

Sophie chuckled but said, "I warn you, I am taking you at your word, Don. Come along."

She led him toward the room set aside for dancing. En route she pointed out the guests of honor—a tawny-haired young man and a breathtakingly beautiful young blonde.

"Now, how did *she* escape my notice?" Everdon murmured.

Sophie's lips twitched. "She hid herself in Chelsea. But she was strictly interested in marriage anyway, so would have had no time for you, Don."

Everdon kept his smile to himself. "Are there many unclaimed hopefuls this year?"

"The usual number, I suppose. I find it rather depressing. Now, let me find you a suitable hair shirt . . ."

Everdon quickly said, "Not Maud Tiverton. Please."

Sophie grinned. "She would wipe away any number of sins, but she is not here."

A set was already in progress, and so the wallflowers were obvious. Most were chattering to friends or chaperones, trying to pretend that this conversation was what they had come for. A few did not hesitate to look bored. One of these was Lady Deirdre Stowe. She sat by her mother, hands in lap, a vacant expression on her plain face.

Everdon had encountered Lady Deirdre any number of times in his mother's rooms, for the two women's interest in embroidery spanned the difference in age, but she had made little impression on him. On his way here he had tried to summon up a picture of her. He knew she was of medium height, and thin. He rather thought her hair was brown. He knew her voice neither appealed nor offended.

Now he studied her more closely. Some effort had been made to pretty her up for the evening, but if anything, it had made matters worse. A fussy pink dress overwhelmed her without disguising her thinness. A confection of curls pulled the hair from her face, emphasizing its angular length and pallor and an unfortunately heavy nose. That hair could not really be called brown, being more the color of weak milky tea.

She was plain, and close to being ugly.

He wasn't repulsed. He experienced instead a spurt of pity, and rejoiced that he was going to brighten her life. He would surely be rewarded by gratitude at the very least.

"It seems a shame to disturb one of those interesting conversations," he said. "Isn't that Lady Deirdre Stowe over there? She's a friend of my mother's. Why not present me to her as a partner."

Sophie Ashby, no fool, gave him a shrewd look. "I remind myself that you have never been known to toy with vulnerable hearts ... Certainly. Lady Deirdre deserves a few more dances."

Lady Harby looked up hopefully as they approached. A flicker of disappointment crossed her plumply amiable face when she saw that Lady Randal had a married man in tow, but then she smiled. When Everdon was presented to her daughter as a partner for the next set, she made no objection.

He took a seat next to Deirdre until the new dance started. Lady Deirdre looked faintly surprised at the turn of events, but not excited. He wondered if she was capable of excitement. He reminded himself that it didn't matter. He intended that she stay quietly in the country, setting stitches and rearing children, while he sought excitement elsewhere.

He addressed a few conventional remarks to her— about the weather, and the recent excitement of the victory celebrations. She replied, but without animation.

He tried a new tack.

"I have seen the work my mother has in hand, Lady Deirdre. It is remarkable. I understand you are encouraging her to see her skills as art. I think you are correct."

At last there was a spark of interest in her gray-blue eyes. "Thank you. I do believe people can be artists with the needle as well as with the brush."

"Needle-painting, is it not called? I have seen the needlework renderings of Old Masters by Mrs. Knowles and Mrs. Linwood. They are very cleverly executed. Is this the kind of work you do, Lady Deirdre?"

Her animation faded. "No, not really."

He was intrigued. "What, then, do you do?"

She looked down self-consciously, and her voice was muffled as she replied, "I create original designs, my lord. Most people do not admire my efforts."

"Why not?" Everdon recognized with resignation that the usual was happening. As soon as he met a sad woman, he felt a compulsion to make her happier in some way. He was distracted by wondering whether the urge would have taken him with Maud Tiverton, a woman whose nature was as ugly as her form.

His companion had said something. "I beg your pardon. The music drowned your words."

She looked dubious, for where they sat, the music was not particularly loud, but she repeated, "I use my needle to create pictures of things other than flowers."

"Surely that is not so unusual. Tapestries have formed scenes of landscapes, people, architecture . . ."

His interest had broken her reserve a little. "My work is not exactly tapestry. I use a variety of stitches." She hesitated, then added, "I am experimenting with the style of Mr. Turner."

Everdon had to admit he had difficulty envisioning embroidery in that sweeping, messy style. He was not an admirer of Mr. Turner's paintings. He made the polite response. "I hope to see an example of your work one day, Lady Deirdre."

Again a dubious look, but she replied conventionally. "I would be honored by your opinion, my lord. I understand you are a patron of the arts."

"I buy what I like, particularly if it is by a young artist. I like to surround myself with beauty, and I hope I occasionally support a struggling new artist who will one day become someone great. See, Lady Deirdre, the set is over. Why don't we walk as we wait for the next one to form?"

She rose without complaint, and he thought she must be glad to leave her station. He wondered if there were any men here he could encourage to dance with her. He had no intention of making her remarkable by dancing with her more than once, but had no desire to see her back in her tedium.

He saw the young Duke of Rowanford talking to another of Randal's cousins, Chart Ashby, and a striking, dark-haired young woman. What a remarkable number of handsome ladies there were in Society when one stopped to look. He steered their way. The men were known to him, and handsome and highborn enough to be flattering dancing partners.

Rowanford raised his brows in surprise. "Hello, Don. Don't often see you at these affairs."

" 'No pleasure endures unseasoned by variety,' " quoted Everdon. "Lady Deirdre, do you know Rowanford and Mr. Ashby?" He performed the introductions and discovered that the handsome girl was Clytemnestra Ashby, Chart's sister. If he was any judge of such matters, and he was, an announcement concerning her and Rowanford would appear any day. Another promising bud snatched from his reaching fingers . . .

But this was only a humorous thought. He knew he had settled on Deirdre Stowe.

"Lady Deirdre is a dear friend of my mother's," he said. "They share an interest, nay, a passion, for the art of embroidery."

He saw Deirdre register the word "art" with pleasure, and the men take in his message that he wanted them to be kind to her. They both requested dances, and Lady Deirdre, flustered, accepted. After a few moments' chat, the music started and he led her into the set.

At the beginning she danced rather stiffly, but Everdon soon suspected that Lady Deirdre Stowe could be a beautiful dancer. He set himself to draw out her talent by distracting her from self-consciousness. Then, when they were together, he subtly urged her into more fluent movement. Slowly she was transformed. She surrendered to the music. She became light on her feet and moved the whole of her body in a supple way most pleasing to the eye. At the end of the dance he was rewarded by an unselfconscious, delighted smile, and noted that the healthy flush of exercise improved her looks considerably.

"That was most enjoyable, Lord Everdon," she said, "You are a skillful partner."

"You are a natural dancer, Lady Deirdre."

She demurred but did not make extreme denials. She was, he thought with approval, a young woman of admirable common sense.

He noted that others had seen her performance, and that when Rowanford claimed the next set, it was with genuine enthusiasm.

Everdon moved on, content with the first moves of the game. He was already thinking of Deirdre Stowe as his own, and planning her welfare and improvement. With a simpler, lighter gown and a more natural hairstyle, she would do quite well in any circle. He had no problem with her behavior at all except for a certain diffidence, which would surely fade when she found herself mistress of her own establishment, secure and valued.

He didn't want to mark Lady Deirdre out with his attentions, and so he had Sophie present him to two other young ladies. It soon became clear to him why they were languishing unwanted. One chattered nonsense in a way bound to drive a man to drink; the other had a hard, bony angularity of body that was most unappealing, especially as he suspected it came out of an anxious temperament that approached the insane. It was quite different from Lady Deirdre's delicate thinness.

His instinct to help twitched in both cases, but he suppressed it.

When he finished the third set, he moved apart to observe the scene, while talking with Randal and Sophie. He smiled wryly when he saw Deirdre taken out for another set by a gentleman unprompted by him. It would be ironic if she found a rival suitor through his meddling. She did look rather more appealing than she had when sitting steeped in tedium.

Success breeds success.

"Pray, why are you staring at Lady Deirdre?" asked Sophie.

Everdon turned to her. "My mother asked me to see if I could liven the last weeks of her Season."

"You've certainly enlivened this evening. If you weren't a married man, I'd wonder about your intentions."

Everdon hoped he didn't show how that had found a mark. "I suppose she would make a tolerable wife, if a man were looking for such."

Sophie wrinkled her brow. "Tolerable? How dull. But I'm afraid people like Lady Deirdre do not show well in London. She doubtless will do better at home now she's spread her wings. Lady Harby, however, has a bee in her bonnet about good matches. She's married the three older girls brilliantly and is determined to do the same for the last. Foolishness, of course."

Everdon glanced at her. "You don't think Lady Deirdre can make a brilliant match?"

Sophie was taken back. "You're pushing me into sounding mean-spirited, but no, I don't. She simply has no remarkable feature and is rather plain."

"Oh, you are doubtless correct," Everdon said amiably, and took his leave.

2

E verdon considered matters carefully, and decided there was little point in delaying before
making his offer. To woo Lady Deirdre might raise
expectations beyond those he felt able to fulfill, and
besides, he couldn't woo her publicly without revealing his widowed status. He would much prefer to be
spoken for when that news broke.

He duly presented himself at the Harbys' hired
house the next day, and was soon closeted with the
earl. Lord Harby didn't hide his surprise and delight
at the turn of events.

"Wife dead, hey?" said Harby, a plain country man
who would never leave his acres if he had the choice.
"And six months ago, too. Well, if you're for making
a sensible match, you won't do better than Deirdre.
Very sound head on her shoulders, has Deirdre."

"So I think, my lord. You have no objection, then,
to my pressing my suit?"

"Objection?" said the earl, rubbing his hands. "Not
at all. Delighted. That'll be the last of 'em, and with
any luck, I'll never have to join this circus again.
Worse than usual this year, with foreigners all over
the place, and the ragtag of the world come to gawk.
Fêtes in the park, indeed ... But come now, let's just
get business out of the way."

Lord Harby had a sound head on his shoulders,
too, and the experience of marrying off three daughters already. Settlements were soon outlined and

agreed to that would ensure his youngest daughter's security. Everdon agreed to everything without debate.

"Excellent, excellent." Lord Harby poured them both wine, and they toasted the coming union. Then he sent for his wife.

Lady Harby came close to palpitations when she realized what was afoot. "Oh my, oh lud! Didn't I *tell* you, my dear Harby, that someone suitable would see the worth of our lamb? I *knew* it must be so. Oh, I am so happy. Four daughters all well set in life!"

Then, disconcertingly, the fluttery manner dropped away and she fixed Everdon with eyes that were no longer vague. "I must say something, however ..."

"Now, my dear ..." Lord Harby interrupted uneasily.

"No, Harby, I will have my say." She remained a plump woman dressed in a very silly manner, but there was nothing silly in her expression. "Lord Everdon, I am a plain woman, and stand no nonsense where my chicks are concerned. You are known as Don Juan, and not without reason."

Everdon stiffened under this attack, for he had not expected it. "Indeed," he said rather coolly. "Such a sobriquet is to be expected when I have a Spanish mother and foreign names."

Lady Harby sniffed. "That has nothing to do with it, as all the world knows. You name comes from that lewd Spanish poem, and is well deserved. Don't seek to flummery me, young man, for I'll not have it."

Everdon was strongly tempted to say that she could keep her damned daughter if that was her mood, but along with the outrage came some admiration. If daughters turned out like their mothers, he was pleased to find some backbone in the stable.

"You refer to my many lovers," he said frankly.

Red flags appeared in Lady Harby's cheeks, but frankness did not deter her. "I do. And I tell you straight, I won't have my daughter made unhappy by scandalous gossip."

Everdon took a calculated pinch of snuff, then dusted his fingers. "As I wouldn't want my wife to be made unhappy by scandalous gossip, Lady Harby, I think we are in complete agreement. May I see Deirdre now and put my case to her?"

Lady Harby looked as if she would say more, but her husband stepped in quickly. "I'm sure Everdon will do all that is proper, my dear. Come along, my lord. Deirdre will be in her little room at her stitchery. One thing's for sure, you'll never lack for a good chairback or a neatly sewn pair of slippers . . ."

It was not to be quite so easy. A hissing conversation developed between the parents, of which Everdon pretended polite ignorance. He heard Lord Harby mutter, "She'll look well enough, Lady Harby. Looks better before you get your hands on her, in my opinion!"

Then Everdon was shepherded across the hall to a small but pleasant room with excellent light where Lady Deirdre Stowe sat working at an embroidery frame. He gained an immediate impression that Lord Harby was right—she looked better unfussed-over. Her plain white muslin, and her hair looped carelessly on her head with tendrils escaping, became her much better than elaborate styles. It still didn't make her anything but a very plain young woman.

She looked up, surprised. "Father? Mother? Why, Lord Everdon, how pleasant to see you."

His lips twitched. Despite her polite words, Lady Deirdre was clearly put out by the interruption.

Lord Harby rubbed his hands nervously. "Good morning, Deirdre. Here's Everdon come to see you."

She stood. "How kind. You have a message from your mother, my lord?"

Everdon heard the door close behind the retreating parents, and saw her eyes widen. She was naturally pale, but he would swear she grew paler. Shock. Better get on with it.

"Lady Deirdre, I think you have guessed my purpose. I wish to make you an offer of marriage. I have your parents' blessing, but it is your consent that counts. You may think we do not know one another very well, but I have observed you, and I am sure you are everything I wish for in my life's companion."

Her mouth worked, and then she said, "But you are already married!" It sounded strangely like a cry of relief.

"My wife is dead. She died some time ago, though the news is recent."

Deirdre Stowe sat back upon her chair with a thump. How could this be happening when she'd thought everything safe? How could this stupid man be ruining her life like this? She wanted to rage at him, but sought some more subtle approach.

"Even if your wife died some time ago, my lord, it would cause a deal of talk for you to marry again so soon after the news becomes known."

"Talk doesn't bother me. If it bothers you, Lady Deirdre, the wedding can be delayed for some months."

The sense of imminent danger retreated, and Deirdre took a deep breath to steady her whirling head. There had to be a way out of this. She looked up at him, looked closely at him for the first time.

She'd seen the Earl of Everdon occasionally during her visits to his mother, but not very often. As she had considered him of no consequence in her life, she had not studied him, though she had to admit that his reputation had always fascinated her.

What made a man irresistible to women?

He was, she supposed, very handsome. His parts were well formed and put together perfectly, but his claim to attractiveness must also come from less definable things, she thought—his ease in movement, and an expressiveness in his features. Even now she could detect the ghosts of humor, warmth, and something else remarkable that she could not pinpoint.

Whatever it was, she wanted no part of it.

She raised her chin. "I cannot imagine how you can think you know me well enough to propose this step, my lord."

"You will allow me to know my own mind, Lady Deirdre. I know enough."

"How, pray?"

His brow raised at this bluntness. "My mother speaks often of you."

"And that is a basis for marriage? I confess, my lord, I am shocked."

He came toward her, dark eyes far too knowing. "And not pleased, I think. Why?"

His arrogance snapped her patience. "Why on earth *should* I be pleased?"

"Lady Deirdre," he said with an edge, "let us not fall to squabbling. If you do not want me, you have merely to say so."

"Oh, have I? And how do I explain that to my parents?"

He sat in a nearby chair and crossed one elegant leg over the other. "You could practice by explaining it to me. I believe I have a right to that, at least."

He looked so completely at home that it offended Deirdre almost as much as his proposal. This was her private place, and he was invading it. "You have no right to anything," she retorted, "but I will tell you, my lord. I am pledged to another."

"*What?*" His surprise rang sharp enough to be insulting, but he covered it by quickly adding, "But your parents . . ."

"They do not approve."

He studied her for a long moment, and she knew

he did not believe her. She wanted to poke him with a bodkin.

"Then marry me," he said lightly. "I won't hold it against you."

The sound that escaped was close to a snarl. "*I* would hold it against you, you oaf. I *want* to marry Howard. I will be *permitted* to marry Howard, but only if no better offer comes along during this season." She glared at him. "I was so *close!*"

Everdon stared at her. No woman had ever called him an oaf. How the devil had a perfectly simple plan gone so awry? He rose to his feet. "There is no need for this unseemly heat, Lady Deirdre," he said icily. "I withdraw my offer. Marry your Howard with my blessing."

She, too, jumped to her feet. "If only I could! If you had had the courtesy to sound me out before speaking to my parents, we could have avoided this. But by my given word I am not allowed to refuse a suitable offer." She paused and eyed him in a way that reminded him forcibly of her mother. "I could object to your loose reputation . . ."

"*Loose!* Lady Deirdre, you go too far."

"Are you denying you've bedded more women than the Regent's drunk bottles of claret?"

He wanted to lay violent hands on her. Another first. "How would I know?" he snapped. "I don't count my women any more than Prinny counts his bottles."

"Both probably mean as much to the user."

He grabbed her bony shoulders. "*Shut up.*"

Deirdre shut up.

Such anger and peril emanated from him that she couldn't have spoken to save her life. His lips were tight and a muscle twitched from the tension in his jaw. His hands were hot on her shoulders, their power just short of pain. She saw him swallow before he spoke.

"Lady Deirdre, I no longer have the slightest desire to take you to wife. I have, however, made my offer to your parents and agreed to the marriage settlements. The only way out is for you to refuse."

"I can't," she squeaked, then swallowed in order to do better. "I gave my word."

He suddenly let her go. Her shoulders felt bruised and her nerves were quivering. She collapsed back into her chair.

He paced for a moment, then spun to face her. "As you said, you could point out my intolerable reputation."

"If my parents were going to balk at that, you wouldn't have come this far, would you? Father will accept almost any offer that gets me off his hands, and Mother is rather a cynic about men." Deirdre summoned a sneer. "She has been known to say, my lord, that the advantage of a rake is that a woman knows the truth, whereas other men merely conceal their behavior."

His lips curled, too. "A charming philosophy."

"Are you saying it's untrue? Among the *haut ton*, at least?"

"I refuse to discuss such a matter. You mind is soiled enough as it is. I repeat, Lady Deirdre, how do we escape this entanglement?"

This was growing worse by the moment, and Deirdre felt perilously close to tears. "I don't know." She heard a betraying waver in her voice.

He stalked over to the empty fireplace, and one hand formed a very daunting fist. Deirdre watched that fist nervously. She had little experience of men other than Howard and her brothers, and none of them had ever been violent around her.

Then the anger seemed to fall away, and the fist became a hand again, looking more fit for gentleness than violence.

He turned to her. "Then the only thing is to go

through with it." He laughed dryly. "Oh, don't look so despairing, Lady Deirdre. I mean go through with the betrothal, not the marriage. We will become engaged to marry, but in view of my peculiar situation, no announcement will be made just yet."

"But, my lord, how will we escape marriage? We cannot put it off indefinitely, and I, for one, do not wish to. I had hoped to marry Howard this autumn."

He brushed aside her fears. "I'm sure I can soon manage to behave in such a way that even your tolerant parents will be happy to allow you to terminate the arrangement."

Deirdre's mind skittered around outrageous possibilities. "What on earth will you do?"

He raised a brow. "Is your mother truly so hard to shock? I will leave it, then, to the inspiration of the moment." A devilish look entered his eyes. "Do you have a pretty maid, Lady Deirdre?"

"No," snapped Deirdre, deeply shocked. "She's forty, and rather sullen."

"Pity, I'll—"

A knock at the door interrupted them. His wicked air dropped from him and he came swiftly over to her side. He pulled a ring out of his pocket, and by the time her parents peeped coyly into the room, he was slipping it onto her finger.

Deirdre was numb with surprise, as much at the chameleon change in him as at his action. Her astonishment was complete when he smiled tenderly and tilted her chin for a kiss.

Deirdre stared into his deep brown eyes, wondering what was the true face of the Earl of Everdon, and aware that she was responding to the meaningless touch of his lips against hers. She immediately armed herself against such a response. She must remember that a Don Juan would be bound to have a powerful attractive force. It meant nothing.

He let her go. She looked down at the diamond on

her finger, knowing she had red blotches in her cheeks. She didn't blush prettily as some women did, but just developed two farcical red stains on her pale skin.

Deirdre was not in the habit of repining over her looks, but at this moment she wished quite desperately that she were pretty. Perhaps then she would know how to handle this muddle with more grace.

Then she realized plans were being made. She put aside her useless musings and paid attention.

"No need to hang around here anymore," said her father with patent relief. "We can get back to Missinger."

Lord Everdon cast Deirdre a tender look. How could he, the wretch? "But you will be depriving me of Deirdre's presence, my lord, and depriving Deirdre of the rest of her Season. It looks to extend well into the summer this year, what with victory pageants and celebrations . . ."

Lord Harby gave a visible shudder. "London's a hotbed of vice and disease," he said, "and all these crowds make it worse. Best to be back in the pure country air, say I. Thing to do is for you to come along, Everdon! Fine chance for you and Deirdre to become better acquainted, and plan your future."

Everdon slanted another look at Deirdre, one that made her shiver with its deceptive longing. "If you insist in taking Deirdre away, my lord, I must assuredly follow. First, however, I must escort my mother to Everdon Park."

Deirdre spoke up then. "Would Lady Everdon care to visit Missinger, my lord? I would be delighted to have her come with us, especially as she is to be my mama." Lucetta, she was thinking, would be a bulwark against this trickster.

"How charming," fluttered Lady Harby with a sigh and a simper. "I, too, would be delighted of the opportunity to become better acquainted with your mother, Everdon."

"I will ask her," said Everdon. "I anticipate no difficulty." He smiled at Deirdre as if she really were the love of his life. "She is already very fond of you, my dear." He kissed Deirdre's hand tenderly before taking his leave.

She didn't know how a man could act a lie so shamelessly.

Deirdre wanted to return to her needlework but had to suffer her mother's excited chatter. Lady Harby was in ecstasies about this unlooked-for success, and busily planning the wedding that would never be. Seeing that her mother was set for a long chat, Deirdre took up her work again and let the words wash over her.

"I knew you could do much better than that Howard Dunstable," said Lady Harby. "How any daughter of mine could be such a widgeon, I'll never know. A hundred a year and no prospects! He would never have made you a good husband, I know it."

And Everdon would? thought Deirdre. How money and title could blind. Howard Dunstable had little money, but he was involved in meaningful, important work, not a search for new debauchery. And Howard needed her.

Deirdre knew Howard would be lonely just now with her here in London. He was probably not eating well, or remembering to change if he was caught in a shower. As a mathematician, he frequently lost track of reality among the numbers in his head.

When Lady Harby began to wind down, Deirdre looked up from her needlework and said, "You must know, Mama, that I do not want this marriage."

Lady Harby was not at all disconcerted. "Yes, of course I know, dear. You still want that Dunstable. But you gave your word, and I'll see you keep it. Trust me in this, Deirdre. Everdon will make you a far better husband than that other one. I'm not willing to let you make a tangle of your life through sheer stubbornness."

"It is not stubbornness, Mama. I *love* Howard."

Lady Harby snorted. "You don't know what love is. I suppose he makes you feel needed. Men sometimes do that. There's nothing wrong with being needed, dear, but there has to be more than that to make a good marriage. Respect, for one thing."

"I *do* respect Howard!"

"Do you? For what?"

"He has a brilliant mind."

"Very likely," said Lady Harby, unimpressed.

Deirdre wished her mother were as foolish as she often appeared. Nothing escaped her at all. "Am I supposed to respect Everdon? He's a worthless rake."

"He is not worthless. He's very rich." Lady Harby overrode Deirdre's scathing comment. "He's also more than that, dear. He's a man who runs his properties well, and speaks intelligently in Parliament from time to time. He's not even a rake in the true sense of the word. Harby assures me he don't gamble or drink to excess. He just likes women. If you do your part, he won't stray much, and I'd judge that he'll always be discreet."

Now it was Deirdre's turn to snort. "How can he be discreet when he's labeled Don Juan? No one will ever believe he's not going from bed to bed, no matter how he behaves!"

"We'll see." But this was a distinctly weak response.

Deirdre pounced on her mother's point of vulnerability. "Mama, I don't want to marry a man who'll go from bed to bed. If he behaves badly before the wedding, will you let me break the engagement?"

Lady Harby looked at Deirdre searchingly, but then she nodded. "Yes, I will, dear. If he's rogue enough to behave badly before you're even wed, I'll admit you're right about him. I'll even let you marry your silly Howard." She rose and smiled confidently. "But it won't come to that, you'll see, which is the only reason I make the promise. Everdon is far too much of a gentlemen to embarrass you in that way, so playing silly games to turn him off won't get you anywhere, young lady."

Deirdre fought not to show her glee. "I wouldn't know how to play silly games, Mama."

"Every girl knows. They come into them like they come into talking and walking. Just remember, you'll be under my eye, so no tricks. September," she said with a brisk nod. "We'll have the wedding in September." With that she bustled off.

As soon as her mother left, Deirdre let out a muted whoop of delight. It was all set! Lord Everdon was as eager to escape this engagement as she, and surely he knew just what to do to disgust her mother. She was even naughtily intrigued as to what the wretch would do. Deirdre giggled at the thought of him trying to seduce Agatha Tremsham, her dresser.

She supposed he'd find a willing dairymaid, or one of the country lasses, and be indiscreet about it.

Then the engagement would be over, and Deirdre would have her mother's permission to marry Howard. She leapt up and did a little dance through the sunbeams. She couldn't wait to tell Howard how perfectly it had all turned out.

Then she halted, thoughtful. Affairs were going to be a little awkward for the next few weeks. She and Everdon would be at Missinger playing the happy couple, while Howard was down in the village feeling neglected . . .

But, she told herself, they could regard it as merely a short trial before total happiness. Thank goodness Howard was not of a jealous nature. He would understand immediately that this was the only path to their wedded bliss, and by summer's end they would be married.

Deirdre settled back to her needlework—a picture of fish underwater done on many layers of gauze. Everything, she thought, was turning out perfectly, and she counted off the blessings in her mind to prove it.

One, if they were to leave London soon, there would be no more excruciating balls and soirées to sit through.

Two, Lucetta would be coming with them, which would mean that Deirdre could continue the only true pleasure she had found in London—her friendship with Lady Everdon.

Three, Lady Harby would keep her word and allow Deirdre to break her engagement and marry Howard.

She nodded. There could even be a September wedding, but not the one her mother planned.

She would not, Deirdre decided with a grin, let Lord Everdon know what a good turn he had served her.

Over dinner and after, Deirdre had to endure yet more excited discussion of her future as Countess of Everdon, but at least she wasn't dragged out to Almack's. She smiled, and let her mother chatter.

When she went to bed, she took off the meaningless diamond ring and tucked it away in her jewel box. If the engagement was not to be announced, she could not be expected to wear it in public.

She climbed into bed, intending to enjoy the planning of her future with Howard. Instead, she found her mind determinedly fixed upon her unlikely betrothed.

Why would any woman want to marry a man with such a notorious reputation?

She supposed the fact that Everdon was an earl would count with some women, and his looks would carry weight with others. Even she had to confess that he had lovely hands. She toyed with the idea of stitching a picture of them—long-fingered, strong, deft . . .

Then she remembered them tight on her shoulders and forming purposeful fists, and shuddered. The man was clearly a bully.

She forced her mind to turn to Howard, who was also very handsome. Howard, however, was a gentle and pure-living man.

Everdon was the complete antithesis. Despite his outrage when she spoke of it, he made no secret of the fact that he went from bed to bed. Some of his lovers were known, some merely rumored. Some, she supposed, were kept discreetly private. She wondered waspishly if he truly was so irresistible when he never stayed with any woman long. Even his wife, it was said, had given up on him after a mere six months.

Perhaps that was it, she thought with a chuckle. He couldn't keep a woman longer than a six-month and thus had to work on quantity. Deirdre covered her mouth. Oh, dear, what with her mother, her friend Anna, and Lucetta, she had developed a rather bold turn of mind. Now, see the consequences. When she'd lost her temper with Everdon, she had said the most outrageous things.

She chuckled again at the memory of his shock and anger. Served the conceited wretch right.

Deirdre rolled over and snuggled down in bed.

Everything was finally going to be perfect.

Everdon decided not to enlighten his mother immediately as to the true state of affairs. She clearly favored a match with Lady Deirdre, and if he told her it was all a sham, soon to be ended, she might try to hold them to it. However, when he broke the news that he was engaged to marry Lady Deirdre, he was surprised by her lack of delight.

"I thought you'd be ecstatic," he said.

"I will be pleased if you deal well together, dear."

"I suppose we will." At her silence, he became impatient. "You suggested her, remember? You can hardly expect me to be in quivers of delight. I scarcely know the girl."

"Quite so."

He swore, but under his breath. "I told you, Mama. It's a lottery. Time will show whether I win or lose. By the way, no announcement will be made as yet. It would be a little crass to announce my widowing and my engagement in the same newsheet, and I must post down to tell Genie's family before making her death public."

At that, Lucetta looked up with concern. "Must you tell them in person, dearest? It will not be a pleasant mission. They have always held you to blame, unfair though that is."

"It is something to be done in person, Mama. I doubt they'll shoot me. After that, I am invited to visit Missinger and continue my wooing of Lady Deirdre. She asked that you come, too, if you feel up to it."

The dowager's eyes glinted with interest. "Clever girl. I would be delighted."

He looked at her warily. "Why clever?"

The dowager merely smiled with all the enigmatic quality of the Sphinx. "You will see."

Everdon sincerely hoped not, and took himself off to his club. He was distinctly uneasy.

He would have been hard put to say what he thought of his strange betrothal. It would delay his plans for his real marriage, which was unfortunate, but on the other hand, it could be amusing to spar with Lady Deirdre for a month or so.

Surprising what she concealed beneath that dull

surface. She was something of a termagant when roused. He supposed he should have realized his mother would not have grown so close to a tepid miss, no matter how strong her interest in needlework. He'd rather like to be a fly on the wall at one of their stitchery sessions, especially if they came around to discussing him.

The thought of Deirdre and his mother conspiring together in the intimacy of a country house did give him pause, however. Perhaps he would be wiser to alert the dowager to the true state of affairs. Otherwise, she might exert herself in his and Deirdre's interest to such good effect that they found themselves shackled for life.

He chuckled at the thought. He would be as content to marry Lady Deirdre now as he had been yesterday, for her lively reaction to his offer had increased rather than diminished her appeal, but he had no intention of taking a reluctant bride. Let her go to her Howard.

Simply to torment her, however, he sent around a note inviting her to drive with him the next afternoon.

Deirdre received the invitation in the spirit in which it had been sent, and planned the outing much like a general approaching an enemy force.

Lady Harby had deplorable taste. In every other respect, Deirdre admired her mother, but it was a simple fact that the lady had no sense of color or design, particularly when it came to clothing. Even in the schoolroom, the Stowe girls had subtly conspired to deflect their mother from the worst choices. When it came to their come-outs, they had been more forceful, despite their mother's complaints that they all liked to dress so dull. Only Deirdre, with her plan in mind, had allowed Lady Harby free rein.

She had been fairly certain that she could survive

a London Season unbetrothed, for she harbored no illusion as to her physical charms, and was intent on behaving as dully as possible. She had made certain of her unpopularity, however, by allowing her mother to choose all her outfits. She now possessed the most ghastly wardrobe in London, probably in all England.

For her drive, Deirdre surveyed her weapons. The green, she thought gleefully. It had to be the green.

She had never actually brought herself to wear this outfit, but clearly remembered the modiste's rather strangled expression when it was ordered. Madame d'Esterville had not been about to object to any part of such a lavish order, but she clearly hoped no one would ever know whence it came.

The walking dress was a striking lime green, bold but unexceptionable in itself, though far too strong a color for Deirdre. Lady Harby had considered it plain, however, and ordered it trimmed with green and white satin puffs, most particularly over the bust to conceal Deirdre's lack of endowments. The striped puffs drew the eye most forcibly to that part of her anatomy, and gave her the appearance of one of those exotic birds that inflated its chest in the search for a mate.

Stilly unhappy, Lady Harby had then commanded the addition of canary yellow mull muslin flounces and collar, and purchased accessories to match.

Agatha Tremsham helped Deirdre into the outfit, but said faintly, "Are you sure, milady?"

"Oh yes," said Deirdre. "I must look my best for Lord Everdon, mustn't I?"

Agatha said nothing. She had been hired at the beginning of the Season, and clearly was resigned to the fact that Deirdre had inherited her mother's taste in clothes.

Deirdre surveyed the complete effect in the mirror. The straw bonnet lined with green and white stripes served admirably to turn her pallor to a sickly green. A green and white striped parasol lined with yellow augmented the effect.

She put on the yellow slippers and mittens, and nodded. "Perfect," she said.

Agatha staggered off, muttering.

When Deirdre walked into the reception room to join Lord Everdon, she enjoyed the glazed look that came over his face, but a second later she saw him recognize exactly what she was about.

Humor glinted in his eyes as he kissed her hand. "My dear Lady Deirdre, I am speechless. I fear I do not do you justice, though. In future, I must try to match you in sartorial brilliance."

She threw him a startled look. Surely he wouldn't really start going abroad in lurid colors?

As he led her to his carriage, he mused, "I'm sure my cousin Kevin has something suitable. Do you know Kevin Renfrew? He has recently acquired the sobriquet of the Daffodil Dandy. It suits him admirably in view of his habit of always dressing in yellow. What a pair you two would make . . ."

Deirdre allowed him to settle her in his phaeton—a very handsome equipage but not, she noted gratefully, excessively high. "Always in yellow?" she queried. "How dull. I prefer to use the full range of the palette. Next time we go on an outing, I must wear my pink and purple for you, my lord."

He settled into his seat, nodded to his groom, and gave the horses the office to go. "I see I shall have to exert myself, Lady Deirdre. Perhaps I should aim for the name, the Rainbow Dandy."

Deirdre found herself unwillingly amused and let a smile escape. Now they were alone, she said, "Pray, don't be foolish, my lord. I wore this outfit to punish you a little, as you well know. You have no cause to punish me."

"Have I not?" he responded. "But if you had not

been so cleverly outwitting your mama, I would never have taken the fateful step of offering you my name. I could happily have been planning my life with Maud Tiverton."

"Maud . . . !" Her eyes met his teasing ones and she laughed. "You truly are a rascal, my lord."

His eyes reflected her amusement. "And you are a minx. Tell me about your Howard."

He turned the team of matched chestnuts smoothly in to the park, but took one of the less-traveled roads. Deirdre felt a frisson of alarm at finding herself alone in the power of Don Juan, but her common sense soon returned. She was the last woman in the world he would try to seduce.

She did not, however, intend to discuss personal matters with him. She looked around instead. "How sad it is to see the state of the park this summer. One would think a herd of cattle had stampeded through it again and again."

"So it has, after a fashion, but a herd of people, not cattle. There were estimated to be a hundred and fifty thousand people here on one day in May to watch the tsar and the king of Prussia ride by. Were you not one of them?"

"No. I can see no appeal in standing in the sun to watch men ride by."

"How dauntingly unromantic you are, to be sure."

Deirdre met his gaze. "Quite." But the effect of those beautiful eyes twinkling with humor almost made a liar of her.

She turned away to frown at the battered remnants of grass and shrubs. "I think it a shame to permit this kind of destruction in any cause."

"Even in celebration of peace?" he asked. "I have no doubt battlefields fare worse. And how can it be stopped? Anyway, I fear that peace—welcome as it is—will mean hard times for the poor, so let them have their moment." He guided the phaeton down toward the deer pound, where the evidence of mass invasion was less obvious. "Now," he repeated, "tell me all about your Howard."

Deirdre did not reply.

At her silence, he glanced over. "There must be something about your devoted admirer that is of interest."

Deirdre looked down at her yellow mittens. "I'm not sure I wish to speak of him to you, my lord."

"Why not? I'm hardly a rival for your hand. I've bowed out, remember?"

Still, Deirdre felt reluctant. No one had encouraged her to talk about Howard. Her mother always became scathing, and Eunice—her sister who lived close by—could not conceal that she failed to appreciate his charms. Even her dearest friend, Anna Treese, had not been able to enter into her feelings.

Lord Everdon would be the least sympathetic of all.

"He is a scholar," she said reluctantly. "A mathematician. He is working on some new calculation which will have great importance."

"Refining the dimensions of the earth by another inch or so, I suppose."

Deirdre raised her chin. "I knew you would sneer. We will talk of something else, if you please."

"I'm sorry," he said with apparent sincerity. "I know little of mathematics. Perhaps during my stay at Missinger I will meet your suitor and have the opportunity to learn."

"That seems unlikely, my lord. My parents do not invite Howard to the house, and in any case, he is far too busy for idle socializing. Anyway, I fear his work would be beyond you." Then she realized that was a trifle rude and glanced at him.

His brows rose but he only said, "Do *you* understand his work, Lady Deirdre?"

Deirdre felt the splotches grow in her cheeks. "Not

exactly. He does try to explain, but I have little background with figures other than household accounts."

"What do you speak of, then?"

Deirdre felt as if she were being interrogated, but she wanted to convince at least one person of how perfect her life with Howard would be. "We plan our life together. He inherited a charming cottage in the village. We will live there, at least at first. It will need a few changes . . ." She racked her brain for more. "I remind him of things, for he is inclined to forget . . ."

Deirdre sighed. It was impossible to describe her time with Howard and convey the truth of it. How could she convince someone like Lord Everdon of her contentment with just sitting and sewing while Howard worked on his calculations? Of how happy she was to walk with him as he spoke of his latest problem, even if she didn't understand it . . .

She stopped trying, and he did not press her. Deirdre relaxed a little and set to enjoying the scenery.

This part of the park was scarcely damaged, and with its spreading trees and deer pound in the distance, could well be the country, so uncivilized did it appear. The leaves were heavy with summer green and formed a barrier to the bustling city. At this time of day, it was largely deserted.

Then Lord Everdon spoke again. "It must be quite delightful for Howard to have someone like you to take care of him, Lady Deirdre. How does he care for you?"

"Of course he cares for me!"

"That is not what I asked."

Deirdre turned to face him. "You have no right to ask me anything."

He stopped the horses, holding them in check with one negligent hand. "Do I not? You wear my ring, Lady Deirdre." He glanced at her gloved hand, which clearly held no rings. "Somewhere."

"It is in my jewel box at home, my lord. Without an announcement, I cannot wear it even if I would."

"Figuratively speaking, you wear my ring," he said firmly. "That gives me some responsibilities."

"It gives you nothing. This engagement is a farce, my lord, and I insist you treat me entirely as a stranger."

"Oh, I think not." He trapped her head with a hand curled around her neck and seared her with a slanting kiss.

It was over before Deirdre had time to react, other than to grow very hot. She scrubbed at her mouth. "How dare you, sir!"

"Don't be foolish. I dare a great deal more than that, but I'm unlikely to go much further without encouragement."

"Which you will never receive," she said hotly. "I give you fair warning, Lord Everdon. Do that again and I'll slap your face!"

A light flickered in his eyes. "You should never warn the enemy. Now I have only to capture your hands before assaulting you."

Deirdre's eyes didn't waver from his. "Then I will wait until I am free. I mean what I say, my lord. Kiss me again and I will hit you with all the power in my arm at the first occasion, even if it takes decades!"

He burst out laughing. "I am entranced! Imagine us, two decrepit specimens lingering at Bath, when you see your opportunity at last. You totter over to my side and tip me out of my Bath chair with a strong right."

Despite her fury, a laugh escaped Deirdre. "I would not have to wait that long, I assure you."

"Of course not." He started the horses again. "I promise when next I kiss you, I'll wait for the retaliation."

A shiver passed down Deirdre's spine. "You won't kiss me again."

"Won't I?"

"If you don't give me your word not to kiss me again, I will never be alone with you."

"Won't that be a little hard to manage with your mother insisting on us behaving as a properly engaged couple?"

"And you would take advantage of that fact?" Deirdre protested.

"I'm sure I will find it irresistible."

Deirdre's hands fisted with anger. "You, sir, are an unmitigated cad!"

Infuriatingly, he smiled at her. "Oh, there must be a mitigating factor somewhere . . ."

She swung at him. He swayed aside and she missed. "You'll have to practice your technique, Deirdre."

They were coming up to a group of riders. Deirdre suppressed the urge to do just that. She put her clenched fists firmly in her lap and looked ahead, struggling to understand how this man could have driven her to attempt violence. She could still feel the power of the desire to do him injury vibrating through her, and she knew he had done it deliberately. He had goaded her for his amusement.

How the devil was she going to survive the next few weeks and remain sane?

3

Deirdre repeated that plea to her friend, Anna Treese, as soon as she was back home in Somerset. Anna's family owned the adjacent estate, Starling Hall, which lay but a two-mile walk from Missinger. Deirdre had rushed over there the morning after her return.

"How will you survive?" repeated Anna, a pretty, dimpled brunette. "What is so terrible about flirting with a Don Juan? Especially as you will get your Howard in the end."

Deirdre caught the sour note in the last sentence. Anna had never made any bones about the fact that she considered Howard a poor candidate for a husband.

"*You* might not mind it," Deirdre pointed out, cradling her teacup. "You've vast experience with flirting, and you've always enjoyed it. I haven't. Compare it to riding, which you do little of. How would you like to be forced to ride a fiery stallion?"

Anna giggled, then hastily steadied her cup. "What a comparison to make!"

Deirdre blushed hot red. "Anna, really!"

"Well, I can't help but have a saucy mind. It's my brothers. They will talk in front of me. And the books they leave lying around . . ."

"You don't have to read them," Deirdre pointed out severely.

"But they're so informative. Have another scone,

dear." She took one for herself. "As for your comparison, *I* am not anticipating a life in the saddle. If I were, I suspect I would learn to like riding the best."

"Well, I am not ..." Deirdre trailed off.

"Anticipating life with a man? Of course you are."

"Howard *is* the best," Deirdre said firmly.

"Really? In what way?"

Why, thought Deirdre, do I always have to justify Howard? "He has a fine mind."

"That won't keep you warm on a cold night."

Deirdre blushed. "He needs me."

Anna shook her head. "Old Tom needs you more. Why not marry him?"

As Old Tom was a lackwit much given to the bottle, this was true and completely irrelevant. "Old Tom is not handsome, whereas Howard is. I'm sure *that* argument carries weight with you."

"More handsome than Lord Everdon?" Anna asked as she topped up their cups.

"In my eyes," said Deirdre firmly. Thank heavens Howard *was* good-looking since that was all anyone seemed to care about.

"Your Howard is well enough," said Anna, adding surprisingly, "though looks are not so important in my mind. I'll grant that Mr. Dunstable has height, and a noble profile, and that his wavy blond hair is very becoming. There's something missing, though, for me at least. I'd rather spend time with Arthur Kealey. He still has spots, poor lad, but he's fun and has a kind heart."

"Has Arthur won your heart, then?" teased Deirdre, deliberately changing the subject. "You always rub along so well."

"Oh no," said Anna practically. "It may just be that he's too young as yet, or that he's not the one. I'm in no hurry. We're all just eighteen," she said, adding pointedly, "None of us need rush into matrimony yet."

"But," said Deirdre triumphantly, "Howard clearly *is* the one for me, for I *want* to rush into matrimony. And it would all be settled now," she added darkly, "if not for Lord Everdon."

"But he's promised to sort it out."

Deirdre put down her empty cup with slightly unsteady hands. "That means he will be coming here, though."

Anna licked crumbs from her fingers and grinned. "Don Juan in Missinger. I can hardly wait."

Deirdre would have willingly waited an eternity for her next encounter with Don Juan, but she knew that could not be. As it was, she spent a great deal of time planning how to limit their encounters to safe locales.

Don Juan, however, caught her in the open, far from cover. So much for careful planning.

Deirdre was strolling down the drive, returning from a flower-gathering expedition, when she heard coach wheels on the gravel. She turned to see a handsome traveling chariot bowling toward her. If she possessed a deeply suspicious nature, she would think Lord Everdon had hovered by the gates all day waiting for just such an opportunity.

The carriage stopped. He opened the door. "May I take you up to the house, Lady Deirdre?"

"Thank you, my lord, but no. I am enjoying the walk."

He leapt down, an image of country perfection in buckskins and top boots, and a great deal more handsome than she remembered. "A stroll after hours in a carriage sounds delightful." He commanded the carriage to go on, then came to her side, a twinkle in his deep brown eyes. "You really should try to look pleased to see me, you know."

Deirdre glared at him. She hadn't seen him since that drive, for she and her family had left London for

Missinger the next day, carrying the dowager with them. He had set off for Northamptonshire to inform Sir Bertram and Lady Brandon of their daughter's demise.

The news of his wife's death had appeared in the papers a few days later.

"I am not pleased to see you," she said flatly, wanting to make the situation absolutely clear.

She set off purposefully toward the house, a good mile away. As she went, she considered tactics. If the underhanded wretch tried to kiss her here, she'd either have to put up with it, or drop her armful of flowers to retaliate. She'd be able to retaliate, she was sure. She had sought advice from Margery Noons, one of the dairymaids. She'd once seen Margery lay out one of the stable lads with a mighty blow.

"You got to swing into it good, milady," the girl advised. "Think like you want to knock their block right off their shoulders."

Deirdre was quite prepared to do just that, but she'd rather it be sometime when she didn't have a mass of carefully selected blossoms in her hands.

"An interesting collection of blooms there," Everdon said amiably. "Let me guess. You have decided to embroider plants after all, and intend a novel assembly of wildflowers."

How did he know that? "I never said I refused to use plant designs."

"Wildflowers after the style of Mr. Turner," he mused. "I look forward to seeing the end result."

Deirdre pounced on that. "You will be gone by then, my lord."

"Alas, it is quite likely. Will you send it to me as a parting gift?"

She glanced at him, startled. "Why should I?"

His smile had a lazy kind of power. "I am going to have to exert myself to free you, Lady Deirdre. Do I not deserve a reward?"

"That depends," she said pointedly, "on how you behave in the meantime."

"Ah," he said with twitching lips. "You mean the kisses."

Alarm shot through her. "I warned you, sir . . ."

He raised his brows. "I thought you would have noted my restraint, Lady Deirdre. I am quite aware that you are under a handicap at the moment, and thus have not attacked. I need no such advantages."

Deirdre could think of no suitable response, and speeded up her pace.

Having much longer legs, he kept up with her without difficulty. "This is a charming property," he said, "and the land about seems to be in excellent heart. I understand your father is very well informed on agricultural matters . . ." He kept up an effortless monologue on agriculture all the way to the house.

Deirdre was relieved not to have to bandy words with him. It was only when they arrived at the house that she realized he had been talking sense. He seemed to know his crops and cattle, and could not be entirely a social butterfly.

His monologue had also allowed her to recover her equilibrium and good manners. She turned to face him. "Here we are, my lord. Welcome to Missinger. I see my parents waiting to greet you. I am a little untidy, however, and need to put these blooms into water, so I will leave you here and use a side entrance."

He made no attempt to stay her, but bowed. "Until later, Deirdre."

Deirdre made herself walk away calmly.

A few minutes later, while she arranged the flowers, she talked herself into sense. "I knew he was coming," she muttered as she snipped stems. "I knew he'd be up to mischief." She worked the pump to fill three vases with water. "Heaven knows why he teases me so. I suppose he just can't help himself." She pushed the poor flowers into their vases rather roughly. "Despite what he says, I needn't be alone with him much."

She washed her hands, glaring at the fragile blossoms. "And if he tries to kiss me," she told them, "I *will* try to knock his block off."

What worried Deirdre, however, was not so much the fact that he would try to kiss her again—it had become a kind of challenge, she saw that—but the alarming response she felt to the prospect. She wouldn't say the challenge was pleasant, but it was *unignorable*.

When she'd explained her strange situation to Howard—and he hadn't seemed to mind—she had tried to get him to kiss her, to substitute one experience for the other. He had not complied. In fact, he'd been rather shocked, and accused her of coming back from London with some very peculiar notions.

He was right, she told herself firmly. Libertines like Everdon might kiss women without a care in the world. Good, decent people waited at least until they were properly betrothed, and probably until they were married.

She rang for a footman, and ordered the flowers taken to her workroom, then went up to her bedroom to change.

The question was, what to wear?

She still had all her London gowns, but having been free of them for a week, she really couldn't face the prospect of wearing them again. Anyway, her two brothers would tease her unmercifully if she did. Consequently she let Agatha choose, and ended up in a very ordinary, but becoming, cream muslin sprigged with rosebuds. Then the maid looped her hair back with a ribbon.

When she joined her family in the drawing room, Deirdre knew she looked as well as possible, and better than Everdon had ever seen her.

She found him instantly, safely talking to her

mother and the dowager. Her father was part of the same group in body, but could not be said to be so in spirit, as he was absorbed in Poulter's *Treatise on Agricultural Management*. Deirdre's two brothers were some way from their elders, joking together and lounging their lanky bodies in a very sloppy way. She joined them.

Her older brother, Viscount Ripon—generally called Rip—greeted her with, "Ain't you going to sit by your beau, Dee? Most women can't keep their hands off him." Rip was a handsome, dashing blond, and just now his grin came perilously close to a leer.

She smiled tightly. "I'm sure he's a reformed character now, Rip."

"Don't know as they ever reform," said her younger brother, Henry. At just seventeen, nearly two years younger than Deirdre, various bits of him had still to catch up to the rest. He showed every sign of following the Stowe tradition, however, and being a danger to the opposite sex. Deirdre knew herself to be the sparrow in a family of showy birds.

Henry was always trying to emulate his older brother, so he essayed a leer, too. "Everdon's strong meat for a little squab like you, Dee, but I'm sure he'll know how to please any lady. Do you think he'd give me a few pointers?"

Deirdre forced a smile. "I suspect he'd give you a facer if you asked."

She felt her tormentor coming before she really saw him, and experienced no surprise when he sat beside her on the sofa. "What a pleasant house Missinger is," he said smoothly to the three of them. If he'd overheard the conversation, he wasn't going to make an issue of it. "Just large enough to be commodious, but small enough to be comfortable. A real home."

That led them safely into a discussion of the house. Deirdre noted how Everdon continued to steer the conversation—to the local landscape, and then into the sporting opportunities in the area. His sophistication and elegant manners made Rip seem almost as callow as Henry. Soon both her brothers were behaving like wide-eyed acolytes and eagerly offering to take him on any number of sporting outings.

When he accepted, she glanced at him in surprise. She'd thought he would devote his time to tormenting her.

His dark eyes twinkled with humor. "You look disappointed, Deirdre. Do you not approve of the chase? Or do you think I should be hunting some other prey?"

"No, please," she said hastily. "I'm sure you will be well suited with blood sports."

"Dee's a bit squeamish about such things," said Rip. "Never have managed to get her out with the hunt, though she's a pretty good rider. Only weighs a feather, of course, but surprisingly strong."

"Really?" said Everdon. "Swings a good right, does she?"

Deirdre choked back a protest, and Henry rolled with laughter. "Not of a pugilistic nature, Dee ain't. Anyway, no female can give more than a tickle."

Everdon focused on him. "I wouldn't take that as a rule of life, Mr. Stowe."

"Oh, really?" Henry sat up, clearly intending to pursue this interesting line of discussion, but Everdon smoothly overrode him.

"If you enjoy riding, Deirdre, I hope you will take me about the estate one day."

Not if she could help it. "If you want a tour, my lord, Father is the one for that. I can't tell a turnip from a mangel-wurzel."

"You can introduce me to the beauties of nature." His voice slid over her deep and soft, as if he spoke of intimate secrets.

Deirdre was infuriatingly aware of her brothers

taking all this in, including her blush. If she continued to protest, they'd remark it, and doubtless comment on it in front of her mother.

"Very well," she agreed ungraciously, but carefully did not specify the day. "Now I wish to speak to your mother. Excuse me, my lord."

He made no objection to her escape.

For dinner that night, Deirdre wore a cerulean blue gown that became her as well as anything. This wasn't by choice, but because her mother had commanded her to put on something particularly pretty. She knew Lady Harby would be content—delighted even—if she were to choose the pink, or the amazing confection of white lace and roses made for her first ball, but she simply couldn't. Her blue, though a year old, still looked well enough.

She rather thought, anyway, that it would be pointless to try to turn Everdon off with tastelessness. He'd kissed her in the green, for heaven's sake, and if that hadn't deterred him, nothing would. The man was clearly set on tormenting her regardless of what she wore.

Perhaps he *was* punishing her. She frowned at her own reflection as Agatha arranged her hair. It would hardly be fair, for he was as much to blame as she for the pickle they were in.

But why would she expect him to be fair?

Strangely, she did.

She added her pearls and went down to dinner prepared for battle, but the meal passed without incident or innuendo.

He had been correct, she thought, in describing Missinger as a home. She was so accustomed that she had not noted it, but here elegance and comfort were pleasingly balanced, and the intention was always that people be at ease. She had been fortunate to be raised here.

She looked fondly at her parents. Her father was wrapped up in his land, and her mother loved garish colors, but they were both wise, kindhearted people who loved their children. It was unfortunate that their one blind spot seemed to be her happiness.

Everdon, she noted, seemed to fit in at Missinger. In this relaxed gathering of people who were comfortable with their situation and one another, he was unobtrusive. She would have thought he would find it boring. Deirdre wondered what his own home was like. Apart from his mother, she did not think he had close family. Then she remembered he'd had a brother, who had died in Spain. At Vittoria, she thought.

For these, and a host of other reasons, she found herself mellowing a little toward Don Juan. He spoke like a sensible man and behaved courteously to all. He had a pleasantly easy manner with her brothers, despite their occasional silliness, and certainly did not encourage them in impropriety. If his words had any effect at all, it would be to steer them into a good way of life.

Nor was there that manner of shocking for effect that she had sometimes observed in men and women with an unsavory reputation; as if they were anxious to prove just how bold they were.

Everdon, she thought, did not appear to be anxious about anything.

Conversation over the meal generally flowed easily, but she noted that if it faltered, Everdon could take any conversational ball and keep it rolling, could find a new one if need be. And this was not, she thought, so much expertise as a desire to make things easy for others. A natural courtesy.

She concentrated on her strawberry flan, wondering why she harbored these strange thoughts. If she didn't take care, she'd find herself liking the wretch.

Perhaps that was his aim, but if he employed such

a method of seduction, it was exceedingly subtle and would be difficult to fight.

Seduction?

Her spoon froze in the act of cutting into crisp pastry. No, even Everdon would not go so far as that in his mischief.

After dinner Deirdre played the piano while her mother and the dowager chatted, both over needlework, though of a very different nature. The dowager was now engaged in a design of birds on fine lawn; Lady Harby was working a geometrical design in tapestry-stitch for a new kneeler for the church.

Despite this difference, they appeared to be rubbing along very well. Deirdre couldn't help thinking how well these two families would blend.

She let her fingers wander over familiar melodies and turned her mind firmly to her future with Howard. She knew little of his family other than that they lived in Leicester, where his father was a solicitor. She rather thought he had mentioned a sister. Doubtless after the wedding, the Dunstables would be invited to Missinger and rub along well, too.

As her husband, Howard would certainly be often at the house. He had not been to Missinger yet, for her mother refused to invite him, but once they were wed, it would be inevitable. She was sure he would fit in.

He wasn't a yokel, after all. Certainly he had little in common with her father or brothers, but they would find something to talk about.

They would have to. They couldn't just sit in silence.

Howard, however, would not linger over his port for hours talking crops and sports, but would come to take tea with the ladies. Perhaps he would sit and watch as she played, or sewed.

She realized she had never played for Howard. He had no instrument at his cottage, and anyway, she visited there rarely, feeling it was not quite proper. Most of their time together was spent outdoors, or at other houses in the neighborhood.

Few of the local gentry invited Howard, however, for he was an unrewarding guest, generally being lost in his numbers. A poet could perhaps be brought to recite his work, but no one wanted to listen to Howard explaining equations ...

Something alerted her. She looked up from the keys and her fingers fumbled into a discord. Lord Everdon was seated on a bench at the end of the piano, gazing at her. She glanced around. None of the other men were here.

He was looking at her in that most disturbing manner.

As if he were enjoying doing it.

She removed her unmanageable fingers from the keys. "Did you want something, my lord?"

He placed his hands—those beautiful hands—on the piano case, and rested his chin on them. "I want many things," he said in a deep, disturbing voice.

Meaningless words to cause her heart to leap into her throat. "I mean, anything I can get for you."

He thought about it. "No. I don't think you can *get* for me anything that I want."

"Some tea," she said brightly, leaping to her feet and heading for the tray. Anything to escape.

He caught her hand as she passed and neatly tipped her off balance down onto the bench beside him. She squeaked, but the other ladies at the far side of the room didn't appear to notice. "What are you doing?" she whispered, jerking her hand free. It tingled, as if she'd just taken part in an electrical demonstration.

"Stopping you from running away. Why are you so afraid of me?"

She folded her hands in her lap and made herself meet his eyes. "I am not afraid of you."

"Then stay and talk to me."

Deirdre couldn't think of a suitable response.

He took her hand again. "I'm hardly likely to kiss you here. What else have you to fear?"

She snatched the hand back. "You are capable of anything, my lord," she said tartly. "You have just manhandled me in public."

"Is that what you call manhandling? It is clear a man has never handled you at all well."

Deirdre raised her chin. "Lord Everdon, you will not speak to me in such a way. It is not decent, and I will not tolerate it."

He smiled. "Bravo! It is pleasing to challenge a spirit such as yours. Pray tell me, Deirdre, how did you endure all those tedious social affairs? I'm surprised you didn't cut your throat—or someone else's."

She was disarmed by his approval, though aware she was likely being foolish. "I plotted designs in my head," she admitted, "though sometimes I amused myself forming couples into unlikely pairs. Little fat Mr. Peebles with gangly Miss Vere. Chatty Lady Hetty with the equally garrulous Lord Tring. Do you think they would kill each other for the chance to speak?"

"More likely they'd both chatter without paying any attention to the other. That's the dreadful thing about the overtalkative. They never listen." He studied her. "And all this was worthwhile as the price of gaining your Howard?"

She felt her face heat and looked away. "Yes."

"Is he worthy of you?"

"Of course he is." She was on edge again, sensing that he had moved to the attack.

"What first appealed to you about him?"

She fixed him with a look. "I have no intention of discussing Howard with you."

"Have you not? But I have this terrible problem,

Deirdre my dear. I take women seriously. I take their welfare seriously. I cannot possibly free you to go to your Howard without being sure he is worthy."

She moved back slightly. "It is nothing to do with you!"

"On the contrary."

"Are you saying you won't arrange the end to our engagement unless it suits you? That is to go back on your word, Lord Everdon."

"I never gave my word."

Deirdre called his bluff. "I don't suppose it matters what you intend," she said lightly. "You are hardly likely to follow a life of purity, are you? I will merely have to wait until you revert to normal, and catch you at it."

He feigned horror, though his eyes laughed at her. "Lady Deirdre, think what you might see!"

"I will *set* someone to catch you," she corrected tightly, knowing the red flags were flying in her cheeks again. "After all, *I* am going to be avoiding you."

"You'll find that remarkably hard to do. Don't forget our betrothal, and your ever-watchful mama."

Deirdre glanced over and saw that even as she conversed with the dowager, and set her neat stitches, her mother had the situation under her eye. Well, Lady Harby knew Deirdre was being forced into this.

Deirdre rose to her feet and simply walked away from her spurious husband-to-be, and this time he let her go.

Shortly afterward, the rest of the men appeared, and Everdon went off to play billiards with her brothers. Deirdre was very partial to the game and would have gone, too, but she knew she'd be wiser to avoid him.

She took up her needlework—a conventional banding for a baby's gown, for she rarely worked on

her more adventurous pieces in public—and joined
the older ladies.

The simple stitches required little attention, and
her mind was free to wander troubling paths. She
foresaw difficult days ahead. There clearly was nothing beyond the boldness of Don Juan.

4

The next morning Deirdre awoke to a visit from her mother. Lady Harby was a somewhat painful first sight of the day, as she had combined an unexceptionable blue-striped cambric with a yellow and brown shawl and a green-trimmed cap.

Deirdre winced.

"It is all arranged," said Lady Harby, as if the bearer of glad tidings. "You are to take Everdon on a riding tour of the estate. Today."

Deirdre sank farther beneath her covers. "Father would do it better."

"Don't be foolish. The man wants to be with *you*, Deirdre. And you are hardly being fair."

"Fair?" asked Deirdre innocently.

Lady Harby gave her a no-nonsense look. "I know you still feel he is forced upon you, but you could hardly do better in the whole of England. He is a charming man. If you would but give him a chance, I am sure he could make you happy with the match."

"He's a rake," said Deirdre mutinously.

"No he ain't. I told you, dear, and we've checked most carefully. He don't gamble or drink to excess, and that's what makes a true rake."

"The whole world knows one thing he does to excess."

Lady Harby looked a little pink at that but said, "You have to give him a chance, Deirdre. It's only fair. He's doubtless ready to settle down."

Deirdre sat up in her bed. "He *kissed* me, Mama."

"Very proper at a betrothal."

"I mean when he took me driving. And it *wasn't* proper."

Instead of showing shock, Lady Harby's eyes brightened. "You can't expect him to be bashful, dear, a man like that. And a few kisses could well show you which way to go." She twitched up her shawl. "Just remember what I've always said—don't let him inside your clothing."

With that, she bustled off to attend to other duties.

Though that phrase had been Lady Harby's oft-repeated advice to her daughters, it flustered Deirdre now. She could all too easily imagine Lord Everdon's long, deft fingers insinuating themselves beneath her most secure clothing. It was just the sort of thing a womanizer would be skilled at.

She had never even considered such a thing of Howard.

Nor, when she came to think of it, had her mother ever felt pressed to repeat that advice to her in respect to Howard.

That surely meant Lady Harby recognized Howard to be an honorable man.

Didn't it?

Deirdre muttered about her ridiculous situation, and rang for Agatha to ready her for the ride. She chose her old dark gray habit, which her mother hated, but which she knew suited her much better than the dragoon-trimmed red ordered in Town.

She did wear the high-crowned shako, however, for it gave her a little height, and she would need all the help she could find to deal with Don Juan. Deirdre pulled on her gray leather boots with pleasure. She liked the feeling of walking in boots, for compared to slippers, they made an impression on the world.

On her way downstairs Deirdre made an impulsive detour to visit the dowager. She hadn't yet told Lady Everdon that the betrothal was false, half hoping that if she ignored it, it would disappear. Lucetta must have guessed that it wasn't a love match, though. Now, faced with the potent reality of Don Juan in her life, it was time to seek Lucetta's aid.

The dowager was still in her bed, addressing a breakfast of rolls and coffee. She accepted a kiss on the cheek and smiled. "That habit suits you, Deirdre. The severe line brings out your strength."

"Strength?" queried Deirdre, perching on the edge of the bed. "I'm not strong."

"Oh, but you are. Not a blustering strong, but strong inside. That's why I think you will suit Marco very well. He needs a real woman to keep him in line. Like my mother with my father."

"Did she have a whip?" asked Deirdre ironically.

Lucetta chuckled. "Not that I know of, but she had a cutting tongue. More than that, she just had strength. He knew she wouldn't tolerate misbehavior, and it held him in check, for he loved her."

Deirdre looked straight at Lucetta. "I don't love Everdon."

The dowager sipped her coffee. "How could you? You hardly know him."

"And he doesn't love me."

"Of course not. Not yet."

"He never will. Not least because this engagement is a sham." Deirdre then explained the whole sorry tale.

Lucetta put down her cup. "Oh, my dear, I am sorry. Why did you not tell me all this? Then I would never have suggested you to Marco as a bride."

"Suggested?" asked Deirdre in surprise.

Lucetta explained her part in it, leaving nothing out.

Deirdre leaped off the bed to pace the room. "So I am a lottery ticket, am I? The wretch! He set out to marry me when he would scarcely have recognized me if we'd met in the street."

Lucetta's lips twitched. "I doubt not that he'd recognize you now, my dear. Why the heat? According to you, it will soon be over. All the same . . ."

Deirdre swung around to face her. "All the same, what?"

"Nothing," said Lucetta mildly. "But if you and Marco are in agreement that you will soon end this betrothal, why are you in such a pelter?"

Deirdre looked away. "Because he's alleviating his boredom by teasing me to death."

"What is he doing?"

Deirdre drew her crop restlessly through her hands. "He . . . he kissed me . . . and he threatened to do it again, even when I told him I'd hit him if he did . . . And he *looks* at me!"

"Looks at you?" The dowager's tone was innocent, but Deirdre turned back and saw the twitch of her lips.

"It's not funny, Lucetta. Last night he was looking at me in such a way . . ." She shivered. "I can't describe it, but it made me most uneasy."

"It certainly can be unnerving to be stared at. I am surprised Marco would be so discourteous."

"It wasn't exactly a stare," said Deirdre quietly. "It was intent. As if I were important . . . as if he *liked* looking at me."

"Perhaps he did. Despite what you think of yourself, you are not hard on the eyes, my dear, especially when you are out of your somewhat strange London outfits." Lucetta sighed. "You must not blame Marco too much for flirting with you, Deirdre. He has inherited the tendency just as he inherited his brown eyes."

Deirdre faced the dowager. "He makes me most uneasy, Lucetta, and it is merely a game to him. Surely he will desist if you ask him to."

Lucetta studied her. "Are you sure that is what you want, Deirdre? It is, after all, just a game, and one he is very good at. I'll stand guarantee that he would never take it too far. Once you are married to your Howard, the time for such games will be over."

Deirdre bit her lip. It was a silly fear, but she worried that in some way this would all prevent her marriage to Howard. "Yes, I want him to stop."

"Then I will do what I can."

When Deirdre left, however, the dowager looked very thoughtful indeed.

Deirdre discovered that Lord Everdon was awaiting her in the stables, and so she went directly there. She came upon him making the acquaintance of Henry's fine gray gelding, and took the opportunity to study the enemy.

He'd been startlingly handsome in evening clothes, and in day wear, but he suited riding clothes, too. The brown jacket and buckskin breeches toned with his skin and hair. They robbed him of some of his fanciful elegance, but replaced it with practical strength.

As if feeling her eyes on him, he turned and smiled a welcome. "Your brother has offered me this fine fellow, Deirdre. I hope your mount will be able to keep up with him."

"Oh, I think so," she said dryly as the groom led out her own gelding, Charlemagne, a black every bit as big and strong as his mount.

She saw the flicker of surprise on Everdon's face, but he came over and tossed her into the saddle without comment. She appreciated the fact that he didn't make any conventionally stupid remarks about Charlemagne not being a lady's mount, or protest that she would not have the strength to control him.

She led the way out of the stables and down a lane

to open ground. "We'll warm them up as we go down to the river, my lord, then have a gallop over to the eastern boundary. I'm afraid we have no romantic features here, though. No monasteries, magic streams, or caves."

Everdon looked around. "Just hundreds of acres of well-tended land. Better than romance any day. I note you do not have much of a park here."

"Mother wanted it, but Father put his foot down. Wouldn't have acres of good land given over to ornamental deer, and artificial lakes and gardens."

"Very wise."

Deirdre glanced at him, aware again that his smooth social manners were disarming her. It was hard to stay wary with someone so courteous. "What is your estate like, my lord?"

He raised a brow. "I have been calling you Deirdre with great boldness. Do you not think you could call me by my given name? We are, after all, conspirators."

She flashed him a look. "Very well. What is your estate like, Don Juan?"

Humor flickered in his eyes. "Don will do. It's what most people call me. Everdon Park, I'm afraid, was extensively improved by my father, but I hesitate to put the ornamental gardens and obligatory deer park to the plow. It's a pleasant place, in fact, but the house is a trifle small. I'm thinking of building an extra wing when I marry."

The word "marry" caused a little frisson in Deirdre, but she reminded herself sternly that she wasn't the bride-to-be. "You should wait and seek your bride's advice on the matter."

"That is my intent."

They progressed along a narrow lane between hedges, heading down toward the river. The sun brightened the scene obligingly, but was not particularly hot. It was a good day for riding. An unwary rabbit hopped into the lane, froze, then darted off. Charlemagne pretended to take offense and sidled. Deirdre saw Everdon come alert, ready to assist her, but he held back, and she controlled the horse without difficulty.

She had to like the fact that he showed some trust in her abilities.

They speeded a little until they came close to the water, silvery-smooth and overhung by trees.

"Your brothers promise me fine fishing," he said.

"They seem to do well enough here."

"You don't care for the sport?"

Deirdre smiled apologetically. "I don't like killing things. I know it's foolish when I'm perfectly happy to eat the trout, or even the roast lamb, but ..."

"It's a foolishness many share. I can't say killing animals is a favorite pastime of mine, though I have no trouble with fish. Or wasps, for example."

"I can't even face the wasps," she confessed. "I trap them and let them free outside. Everyone thinks me very foolish."

"And so you are, but it's a charming foolishness all the same."

Something changed between them. Deirdre couldn't say what it was, but she felt as if a connection had been made. She knew she would never forget him. When he strolled out of her life, there would be a space—a small space, but one that would never adequately be filled by another.

It was most alarming.

He made no other personal comment, however, but looked around. He gestured to a grassy hill a field away. "What is that mound over there?"

Deirdre grasped the subject with relief. "It's said to be a barrow, an ancient burial site. There may be bones inside, or even pots and such. No one has dug to find out."

"And you said you had no romantic features," he

protested. "Can we ride over there? I'd like to investigate."

She obligingly turned and they cantered to the mound, some forty feet long and twenty feet high. The dun-colored cows in the field ambled resentfully away from the invaders.

"I'm going to climb it," he said. "Are you coming?"

"No, I'll wait here." Despite her firm tone, Deirdre couldn't help but remember how much she had loved to be on top of the little hill in her youth. It was hardly an activity for a mature person, however.

He dismounted and tossed her his reins, then went to investigate. Soon he had scrambled up the slope. "It's certainly a man-made shape," he called from the flat top. "If this were my land, I'd get someone in to excavate."

Deirdre suddenly wanted to be up there with him.

Impulsively she slid off Charlemagne, led the horses to the gate, and tethered them there. Then she picked up her skirts and ran over to climb up after him. Halfway up, she discovered that it wasn't as easy as she remembered. Last time she'd done this, her skirts had been shorter, and she'd felt no self-consciousness about revealing her legs. Now her trailing habit tangled her feet, but she couldn't gather it up without being indecorous. She found she was embarrassingly stuck betwixt and between.

He knelt and stretched out a helping hand. After a momentary hesitation, Deirdre took it. His grip was firm, and he pulled her up the last few feet without difficulty, steadied her, then let her go.

Deirdre caught her breath. "Oh, I haven't been up here for years! I used to love to come here as a girl. I felt on top of the world."

"It is not so very high. Perhaps I should take you to the Lakes."

Deirdre hardly paid attention. She stretched her arms out and slowly turned. "I always felt special here. Tall, strong, powerful. Queen of the world . . ."

She kept turning, faster and faster, allowing the world to spin around her and carry her off to dreams . . .

He caught her hands and jerked her to a stop. She fell dizzily into his arms.

"Oh, don't!" she cried.

"You were going to spin off."

The world was still turning around her, but Deirdre said, "Let me go!"

"Wait a moment."

"Let me go!" she cried, panicked by his arms, and the look in his eyes.

He did so cautiously, warning, "If you try to walk, you'll fall over, and end up back in my arms. I'd really have to kiss you then, you know."

She stood there, begging the world to stay still. When she was younger and had done this, she'd collapsed onto the ground afterward and let the sky turn and turn above her. Nothing would induce her to collapse at the feet of Don Juan. "I do wish you'd stop this," she fretted. "You don't really want to kiss me."

"How can you know what I want?"

The world began to settle, and she met his amused eyes. "I'm not the sort of woman you like to kiss."

"Aren't you? In fact, I like to kiss most women."

"That's ridiculous. Do you want to kiss my mother, for example?"

He grinned. "I didn't say I wanted to kiss *all* women. Those that want to be kissed, I want to kiss."

"But I don't want to be kissed. At least, not by you." She ignored his arrogantly skeptical look and added, "Besides, that policy sounds highly dangerous, my lord."

"True, but it wasn't when I was married."

Deirdre nodded. "Ah, I see. And now you are in peril, but like an opium eater, you find you cannot break the habit."

"Precisely. I thought you would be kind enough to let me blunt my appetite by occasionally kissing you, since we are agreed we wouldn't suit."

Perhaps she was still dizzy after all. Deirdre felt most peculiar. Her senses were being deliberately tangled in knots, up here where reality seemed so far away. "But I don't want to be kissed by you," she repeated firmly.

Or at least, she intended it to be firm, but it didn't come out that way.

"Why not?"

"Why on earth should I?"

"It would be fun."

Deirdre took refuge in primness. "Kissing should never be fun."

He laughed. "Now, *that's* ridiculous." He stood, hands on hips, beaver at a jaunty angle, making the world spin again.

"It is not ridiculous," she defended desperately. "Kissing is for holy purposes. For marriage and procreation . . ." She bit off what she had been about to say, realizing where her unwary tongue was leading her. She knew her face was red and wanted to wipe the amusement off his all-too-handsome face. She could see he was trying not to laugh, but his lips were twitching anyway.

"I hadn't actually intended to go so far so fast . . ." he murmured, and walked toward her.

Deirdre pushed him off the mound.

With a cry, he tumbled over and over down the steep slope and lay still.

With a gasp of horror, Deirdre slid and scrambled her way down to his side, not caring if her habit was soiled or her legs were showing. Her heart thudded madly and chills shook her. What would become of her if she'd *killed* him?

She landed by his still body. He didn't look dead, but his olive skin made it hard to tell. Hesitantly she reached to touch his cheek. At the last moment she saw the flicker of his eyelids as he peeped at her.

She leapt to her feet and backed away, her anger returning in full force. "Get up, you wretch. I know you're shamming it!"

With a laugh, he rose and brushed himself off. Then, without warning, he grabbed her, imprisoned her competently in his arms, and kissed her. She tried to kick and twisted her head, but he held her still and laid his lips against hers.

That's all it amounted to, and yet their subtle movements sent a weakness through her. Her limbs lost their strength, her eyes drifted shut, and the world started spinning again . . .

His lips released hers. "Now," he said softly, "I wish to point out that you hit me first. I was merely claiming that for which I'd paid."

Her eyes flew open. "That isn't fair!"

"Is it not? I would have thought I could claim a great deal more for a life-threatening attack like that."

Deirdre decided it would be much wiser to accept his terms. "Yes, damn you, it is fair. Now, let me go."

"Such language," he teased as he released her.

He started to brush off her habit. She pushed him away.

"And that wasn't a hit," she warned him quickly, "so don't pretend otherwise. When I do hit you, Don Juan, you'll know it. I'm going to knock your block off. I've been practicing."

Devil lights appeared in his eyes. "Then I must certainly make sure the kiss is worth the price."

Deirdre wished she'd learn to keep her mouth shut.

She also wished there were a way of getting back on Charlemagne without him touching her, but she had to allow him to toss her into the saddle.

He took no advantage.

What she disliked most about Don Juan, thought Deirdre, was that he was so devilishly upredictable. What would he do, or not do, next?

As they resumed their ride, Deirdre knew she had just escalated their teasing contest. The terrible thing was that she was beginning to enjoy the game.

When she remembered that she'd asked Lucetta to call him off, she actually felt a tickle of disappointment.

Lucetta requested that her son visit her in her room before dinner that evening. He arrived looking carelessly, perfectly elegant and kissed her cheek. "Let me hazard a guess. Deirdre has asked you to tame the savage beast."

She shook her head fondly. "Something like that. Marco, what are you about? She has told me that your engagement is a sham. I confess I am disappointed, but if she has another love, I can accept it. Why cannot you?"

"Do you conceive of me fighting for her heart? Hardly."

She watched him carefully. "Then what are you doing?"

"Amusing myself," he said flippantly, but then sobered. "No, that is not quite honest. It is true that I find it compulsively amusing to challenge Lady Deirdre's spirit. Do you know she is something of a spitfire? I suspect you do. But she is a banked fire. I am just stirring her up, summoning some flames. I won't hurt her."

Lucetta frowned. "Can you be sure of that, Marco? I suspect she is somewhat vulnerable. She does not think too highly of herself as a woman. Lady Harby is in many ways an admirable lady, but her fearsome efforts to turn Deirdre into a beauty have served instead to convince her that she is a hopeless case."

"Then she needs to be shown otherwise. Physical beauty is not particularly important in a woman."

"Strange," mused the dowager. "I have not heard your name linked to any except beauties."

"But what of my more discreet adventures . . . ?" His smile was secretive and, she thought, the kind that would ignite the iciest female heart. It made her want to slap him.

"Don't play your games with me," she said briskly. "I will not tell you to leave Deirdre alone, but I do tell you to watch what you are about with her."

"I don't hurt women, *Madrecita*. Except Genie, of course." Before Lucetta could comment on that, he asked, "Do you know why Deirdre wants to marry this Howard Dunstable?"

"She has hardly spoken of him. Before your betrothal, she never mentioned him or I would hardly have put forward her name. I suppose she must be in love."

He picked up a black silk rose from her dressing table and contemplated it. "Do you really think so? She does not appear to me to be a woman in love. My instincts tell me that he hasn't warmed her soul." He studied his mother, then fixed the rose in the black ribbons of her cap and frowned slightly. "I wish you would wear colors. I remember how beautiful you looked with a red rose in your hair."

"I was more than ten years younger then, dearest. Besides, I will mourn your father all my days, and why would I want to look beautiful except for him?"

He leaned down and hugged her. "So be it. Perhaps I just don't understand the true dimensions of love. As for Deirdre's mathematician, I reserve judgment until I meet him, but I suspect her marriage to him would be an error."

Lucetta shook her head. "How can you make such a judgment, Marco?"

"How can I not? Does she appear to you like a woman afire with love?"

The dowager had to admit that Deirdre didn't. "But, dearest, you must realize some women simply do not have those fires within them."

"Nonsense," he said crisply. "And if there are such women, Deirdre Stowe is not one of them. I am already toasting my toes." At the look in his mother's eyes, he shrugged. "I simply intend to open her eyes to life, so she will look at Dunstable and make a clear-sighted decision. She is far too fine to be wasted on a selfish nod-cock."

"He's supposed to be a brilliant mathematician," she pointed out.

"Perhaps he is, but in all other ways I am sure he is a nod-cock."

Lucetta turned away to hide her amusement, and some burgeoning hopes. "But think, dear. If you should manage to shake Deirdre free of her attachment to this man, what can you do but marry her yourself?"

"I wouldn't mind," he remarked carelessly. "She still seems as good a choice of bride as I am likely to find."

"Quiet, plain?" Lucetta queried. "An adequate lottery ticket?"

He grinned. "Well, plain at least. And highly likely to win me at least a minor prize in the lottery of life."

As he escorted her down to dinner, Lucetta enjoyed the realization that her handsome son was experiencing the first twitches of jealousy. It was so strange an emotion to him that he hadn't even recognized it as yet.

5

The next day Deirdre took swift action to ensure she couldn't be dragooned into another outing with Everdon. She rose early and announced she was visiting Anna. The truth was, she intended to visit Howard "on the way." She needed a practical antidote to Latin charms, and the three-mile walk to the village of Missinger St. Mary would not come amiss either.

Her mother had never made objection to her visiting Howard as long as his housekeeper was present, and Deirdre chose to assume that the rules had not changed. She knew that the latest housekeeper, Mrs. Leadbetter, was likely to be there. The taciturn woman never left the house except on market day.

It was this matter of housekeepers that had first brought Deirdre and Howard Dunstable together.

They had met at a musical evening at the Durhams', where she had seen him sitting alone. Deirdre was not in the habit of approaching handsome young male strangers, but she felt sorry for his isolation and so sat beside him and engaged him in talk. She discovered he had just moved to Missinger St. Mary, where he had inherited a cottage from an uncle. The uncle had also left Howard sufficient income to pursue some mathematical inquiries close to his heart.

That evening he had even attempted to explain his work, but she hadn't understood much of it. It had been a relief when he'd turned to more everyday

matters and told her of his difficulty in finding a
good woman to cook and clean for him.

His uncle's housekeeper, Mrs. Islip, was apparently
most unsatisfactory. Deirdre had eagerly offered to
help. There had been no thought of romance in her
head, just kindness and the reward of being useful to
such a gifted man.

Her first step had been to try to work out the problems between Pammie Islip and Howard, for Pammie
was known to be a good worker. Deirdre persuaded
them both to stick with the situation for a while, and
encouraged Pammie not to sing or chatter when
Howard was working. She began to make frequent
visits to the cottage to see how matters were pro-
gressing and to give Pammie a chance to gossip.

She came to value her visits to Foote's Cottage
very much indeed.

Sometimes Howard was deep in his work, and so
she did not disturb him. Sometimes, however, if he
was pondering matters in his head, he could be persuaded to take some exercise, thus allowing Pammie
to sing as she scrubbed. Usually on these occasions
Howard would talk to Deirdre of his work—not con-
versing, but thinking aloud. Deirdre did not mind.
By listening to his musings, she began to understand
a little more about his studies; enough to convince
her that she was in the company of a genius. It made
her feel so useful and important to take everyday
cares from his shoulders, and then, of course, he
asked her to marry him.

The subject had arisen on one of the occasions
when she'd persuaded him out for a walk. They had
been walking through a field of playful lambs on a
perfect spring day, walking in silence, for Howard
had been lost in the numbers in his head.

But then, perhaps he had not been working
through equations, for he had suddenly said, "Do
you know, I think we should marry."

Deirdre had been startled but thrilled. She had said something silly, like, "Oh, Howard!"

"Good. You're a very useful person to have around." Then, disconcertingly, he returned to his calculations and did not mention the matter again.

A few days later Deirdre reminded him of his words, but tentatively, thinking they might have been a fevered dream.

"Yes, of course," he said. "What's the matter? Have you changed your mind?"

"No. But, Howard . . . if we are to marry, you must speak to my father."

He appeared more concerned with the search for a particular piece of paper than with her words. "Surely you can do that, Deirdre."

"Tell my father we want to marry?" she said blankly.

"Yes. Why not?"

"But he'll want to speak to you about it."

"Why? You can tell him all the details. My income is just over a hundred pounds per annum and I own this cottage. I assume you have a portion, but if you want it tied up for your use and for any children, I don't mind."

Deirdre was thrilled at this evidence that he wasn't marrying her for her money, but protested again. "It's not how these things are done, dearest . . ."

"Forget it, then," he said testily. "Where is Babbage's letter? Has that damned woman been meddling in here again?"

Deirdre was taken aback, but was definitely not about to forget it. She had finally found her destiny and life's work; she was to be helpmeet to a modern Newton.

That night she awkwardly informed her parents of the matter only to see the notion firmly squashed. Her father, she rather thought, would have gone along if Howard had come up to Missinger and stated his case. Her mother, however, was dead set against it.

"I know you've been hovering about him, and I haven't interfered, Deirdre. I judge you to have the sense not to go wrong. Marry him, though? He's a lawyer's son with a hundred a year."

"I love him, Mama."

"Nonsense. He's just the first man to pay you any interest. Creeping around as you do in white and gray, no one even sees you. We're off to London in a few weeks. With some nice bright clothes, and a bit of a push, we can do better than Mr. Dunstable."

Begging had not moved Lady Harby one inch, but so confident had she been of Deirdre's coming success that Deirdre had been able to strike the fateful bargain—that if she returned from London unengaged, she could marry Howard.

Even Howard had admitted it to be a clever plan, and everything had been in hand until Pammie Islip's patience wore thin. Another opportunity presented, and so she gave her notice the very week before Deirdre was to leave for London.

With so little time to find a replacement, and Lady Harby demanding Deirdre's attention for other matters, Deirdre was forced to settle for Nan Copps, though she feared the woman would not do. Everyone knew Nan was a slovenly worker. As feared, Deirdre had returned from London to find Mrs. Copps had moved on to other pastures, muttering about unreasonable buggers.

Howard had been scathing about the woman's inadequacies and quite helpless to cope on his own. It was doubtless this domestic crisis that had muted his reaction to Deirdre's mock betrothal; he was much more concerned about edible food and clean floors.

It had been a blessing from heaven that Mrs. Leadbetter had been looking for a place, old Colonel Grieve having finally died. Mrs. Leadbetter had an excellent reputation for hard work, won prizes for her cooking, and was known far and wide for her taciturnity.

Deirdre felt that at last she had accomplished her task. When she thought that in weeks she would be free of Don Juan and have won her mother's consent to her marriage to Howard, she could not imagine how life could be sweeter. She sang as she walked down the village street, and waved cheerily at the blacksmith, who was taking a moment away from the heat of his forge. He grinned and touched his forelock.

Foote's Cottage was a square stone building fronting onto the main street of Missinger St. Mary, with a long garden in the back running down to the river. Bert Rawston took care of the garden, and it showed a riot of flowers, herbs, and productive vegetables. Deirdre was quite proud of talking Bert into doing the extra work, for he had a number of gardens in his care. Howard, she feared, scarcely noticed how lovely his garden was, for he was not an outdoors person. Perhaps she should point out to him that all the delicious fresh vegetables served up by Mrs. Leadbetter were the results of Bert's skill.

With Bert and Mrs. Leadbetter, and Jessie Cooper doing the laundry, Deirdre knew she had made Foote's Cottage a perfect home. She looked forward to living there one day soon.

There was a handsome green front door with a porch over it, but Deirdre went down the side path to slip in the back door. She snipped a spray of mint from the plant by the door, and bruised it between her fingers for the aroma.

Sinewy Mrs. Leadbetter was in the kitchen, scrubbing a pot.

"Good morning, Mrs. Leadbetter. Isn't it a beautiful day."

"Aye, it is, milady," said the woman sourly. "You'd think some folk would go out and enjoy it."

Oh dear. Deirdre took another fortifying sniff of the mint. "Mr. Dunstable does become caught up in his work, I'm afraid. Perhaps I can tempt him out for a walk."

"See if you can, if you please, milady. I've not been able to dust that room for three days."

Oh, poor Howard, thought Deirdre. He really must take better care of himself.

She tiptoed through to the front parlor, which was now called his study, and found her beloved hunched over his desk. He was a tall man, but she feared his study posture would soon rob him of some of his height. He pushed his hand into his honey brown hair to hold it away from his eyes. His hair really did need to be cut, but it wasn't a matter Deirdre could arrange for him. Not, at least, until they were married.

In fact, she rather liked his hair long. It seemed dashing and piratical. She often thought of running her hands through it, and once or twice she had found the nerve to touch it.

The hands holding his hair back and wielding a stubby pencil were broad, with spatulate fingers. They had always impressed her as strong and practical, but now, disconcertingly, a vision of long brown fingers intruded; strong hands pulling her up to the top of the barrow . . .

She coughed.

Howard looked up with an angry scowl on his square-jawed face, but then it lightened. "Oh, hello, Deirdre. I thought you were that woman. I'm glad you're here. I can't seem to make her understand how I like my eggs."

She smiled and walked over to him. "Poor lamb. I'll speak to her."

"I don't think she'll suit, you know. She doesn't

seem to pay attention to my wishes at all. Perhaps you should find someone else."

Deirdre kept her smile with an effort. "I'm not sure there is anyone you'd like better, love. Just be patient. Once I've disposed of Don Juan, we can be married and I'll manage your life to perfection."

He rewarded her with a smile, one that crinkled the corners of his blue eyes in a very appealing way. "I know you will. Has he turned up yet?"

"Yes, two days ago."

"How long do you think it will be before you can break the engagement?"

"I don't know. Unfortunately, it's up to him to do something embarrassing."

"You could always go off somewhere with him and then cry rape."

Deirdre stared at him. "Howard, I could never do such a thing!"

"Don't see why not. Everyone would blame him, and you wouldn't have to bother about your reputation because we'd get married. If I didn't hold it against you, no one else would. I really can't stand Mrs. Leadbetter much longer."

Deirdre was appalled by his plan, though touched by how much the poor lamb needed her. That was it, of course. This must all be so hard for him. And he frequently didn't really think of the implications of his words unless they were to do with mathematics.

"We'll have to keep her on, even when we're married, Howard," she said. "But I'll be here to manage her for you."

"I suppose that will have to do."

Deirdre sighed. It was terribly stuffy in the room, for he would not have the windows opened because of the noise from the street. No wonder he was out of sorts. There was also a film of dust on the woodwork that must offend Mrs. Leadbetter deeply.

"It's a lovely day, Howard," she said brightly. "Wouldn't you like to go for a walk?"

He glanced out of the window, appearing surprised to see the sun. "Yes, I suppose. Let me just finish this . . ." He turned back to his papers.

Deirdre sat quietly to wait, taking her needlework from her reticule. The baby's gown again, one intended for her sister Susan's next child. As she worked, she drank in the peaceful intimacy and imagined that she and Howard were already married, and that this work was intended for her own child. How lovely this would be.

Or at least, it would be lovely on a cold winter's evening, with a big fire roaring in the grate. Today really was too fine a day to waste indoors. Poor lamb. He worked too hard.

Howard did look wonderful poring over his papers, though, a sunbeam touching his hair to gold. Deirdre wished she had a talent for portraiture. He was in shirt-sleeves, as he usually was to work in warm weather, and wore no cravat. His hair was tousled and curled against his collar.

Definitely piratical.

She noted with concern that he was growing a little pudgy and round-shouldered from so much bookwork. She must tempt him to more exercise. If only he would ride, but he had no taste for it. He didn't shoot, or fish. Not that angling gave much exercise, but it would get him out in the fresh air. Cricket? No, she could not imagine it.

He showed no sign of breaking from his work soon, and she wondered whether she dared remind him she was here.

He was scribbling notes, and checking them against other sheets. She knew if she looked, they would be covered by incomprehensible squiggles. She had asked him once to explain them, but he had assured her it was impossible that she understand.

She had always thought herself good at numbers until she'd met Howard. Numbers in Howard's world were something far removed from anything she had learned in the schoolroom.

He was constantly engaged in communication with three other mathematicians, in a kind of friendly rivalry, and he had presented his work to learned gatherings and written about it for publication. Most people in the area did not realize the caliber of person they had in their midst.

Deirdre had certainly never dreamed of marriage with such a man.

The ticking clock told her she had been sitting here for nearly an hour, with Howard showing no sign of leaving his work. Food might do the trick. She tiptoed out and helped Mrs. Leadbetter to make up a tea tray. As she did so, she tried to mediate on the eggs.

"It's more than a body can manage, milady," the woman stated. "They must be boiled. Not a scrap of the white must be runny, and not a scrap of the yolk must be 'ard. How's a body to tell? And besides, anyone who knows anything worth knowing knows that new eggs cook different from old. How's a body to tell?"

"Perhaps he would take them poached, Mrs. Leadbetter."

"Not 'im," said the woman, with a marked lack of respect. "'As to be boiled. And toast with no scrap of black on it. How am I, all alone, to watch the eggs and 'old the toast, and never get a touch of black? Do you know, he won't eat bread? He reckons the toasting makes it easier on the stomach. I don't know where he gets all these notions."

Deirdre sighed as she picked up the tray. "Please do your best, Mrs. Leadbetter. Perhaps we can hire a girl to help you here."

As she made her way back to the study, Deirdre

wondered whether it was true that toast was more digestible than bread. She was sure if Howard said so, it must be. How strange.

She put the tray down on a table near his desk, braced for irritation. But when he looked up, he smiled. "Do I smell fresh scones? Lovely lady."

Deirdre wasn't sure if he meant Mrs. Leadbetter or herself, and chose not to ask. She poured the tea as he liked it, with very little milk, and basked in his approval. "Please try to be more flexible about the eggs, Howard. Think of Mrs. Leadbetter's baking. She wins awards every year for her pies."

He rubbed his nose and gave a disarming grin. "They are very good. I'll try not to be a bear. It's just that a satisfactory breakfast sets a man up for the day."

Deirdre smiled back, feeling mistily that everything was perfect after all. "When we're married," she promised, "I'll cook your eggs myself." She didn't let the fact that she'd never boiled an egg in her life weigh with her at all.

She received another approving smile and became happily lost in visions of serving him perfect eggs, and baking perfect cakes, and receiving perfect smiles . . .

When Howard finished his tea, however, she found she still could not persuade him to a walk, and had to take her leave. Very daring, as she passed his seat, she leaned down and dropped a kiss on his cheek.

He caught her hand. "You into this kissing business?"

Deirdre went red. "Well, as we are engaged . . ."

"I suppose." He cupped the back of her head with his strong hand and pulled her down. His lips were hot and wetly parted, and the pressure on her neck hurt.

He let her go, and grinned. "There. I don't want

you thinking I'm a cold fish, not with a Don Juan creeping around and pestering you. Off you go."

Deirdre left the cottage in a daze.

He was jealous. That was wonderful.

She hadn't liked that kiss.

That wasn't wonderful.

It had just been the position, she told herself. He hadn't realized how awkwardly he had pulled her head down to his. Next time, hopefully, they would be in a better position. Standing, sitting, lying . . .

Her mind strayed to the marriage bed and she felt distinctly uneasy. That, she told herself, was normal for an innocent young maiden. It was quite possible Howard was an innocent, too, which would account for his clumsiness. They would learn about it all together.

With that settled to her satisfaction, Deirdre went off to visit Anna, so that her excuse for absence would not be entirely spurious. She found that Anna had driven into Glastonbury with her mother, however, and so turned her steps home.

What a shame she hadn't been able to drag Howard away from his books and papers. It was a lovely day for a walk. The sky was clear, but a breeze cooled the air. Summer was at its best and flowers rioted everywhere, filling the air with perfume. Even the tang of the dung spread in a nearby field was a good country smell. Insects hummed about their business, and birds sang all around. Every one of God's creations, including Deirdre, was happy to be alive.

She strode over the fields toward the house, singing along with the birds, planning her happy future.

Then she heard hoofbeats.

She knew who it would be without looking, and turned with a shiver of unease.

He was cantering toward her on the gray, a welcoming smile on his face. But then he kicked the horse to speed.

In seconds, he was charging at her like a cavalry officer!

With a gasp, Deirdre backed up a few steps, but she was in an open field. It would be ridiculous to run. He surely wouldn't ride her down . . .

Deirdre held her place, her heart in her mouth. He held the horse straight at her.

At the last minute, he let go of his reins, swayed sideways, and scooped her up.

She screamed as everything whirled around her, then she found herself perched in front of a laughing Don Juan as his horse cantered onward.

She hit out at him. "You crazy fool! Who the devil do you think you are? The hero of a Minerva novel?"

His teeth were wonderfully even and white as he laughed out loud, "I'm Don Juan! I've always wanted to do that. Of course, it would be even better if there'd been a dragon poised to devour you."

Deirdre growled as she struggled to arrange her skirts with decency. They were all over the place, showing her shift, her stockings, and even a glimpse of a garter. "If there was a dragon, I'd feed you to it," she snapped. "Put me down, you idiot."

He made no move to obey, but he slowed the horse. "I think dragons are only interested in virgins."

Deirdre glared at him. "Put me *down!*"

"No. I'm taking you home."

"I have legs, Lord Everdon."

He looked down and grinned. "So I see."

Deirdre gritted her teeth and wriggled harder until her skirts were decent. "A *gentleman*, my lord, would not have remarked on that fact."

"True, but he still would have enjoyed the view."

"In fact, a *gentleman*," continued Deirdre, "would

never have thrown me over his saddle bow in the first place."

"No? It seems to happen a lot in books. But if you were truthful," he pointed out, "you'd acknowledge that I didn't. Didn't you appreciate the skill in the way I landed you right side up?"

"No." Deirdre looked away and tried to pretend this ridiculous performance wasn't happening, that he wasn't even there. The attempt was futile when she was sitting on his hard thighs and his arm was strong about her.

He spoke softly into her ear. "Perhaps we should do it again, so you can admire my technique."

"Once you put me down, my lord, you'll not have the chance to capture me again."

He laughed. "I'm almost tempted to see what means you would use to avoid it. But discretion prevails. I have no doubt you'd succeed. I think you would succeed at anything you set your formidable mind to."

This casual praise so overwhelmed Deirdre that she relaxed against his chest. "Good, for I have set my mind to marrying Howard."

The were approaching the stable lane. "Were you off visiting him then?"

"Yes."

"And singing on the way home. He must have made you happy."

"He always makes me happy."

"Lucky man," he said softly, almost wistfully, his breath brushing warm over her cheek. She could not deny that it sent a shiver down her spine. She told herself that to be in the same situation with Howard would give her even greater pleasure.

They were just short of the stable yard gate when he halted the horse. Before she could act to evade it, he captured her chin, and a light kiss tickled her lips. "You did hit me," he said.

"Under great provocation."

But Deirdre wasn't angry. She thought perhaps Everdon was coming to understand just how she felt about Howard. When he really understood, she knew he would cease his teasing and leave her alone.

That afternoon Lord Everdon sought a word with Deirdre's mother. He was coming to understand Lady Harby and admire her shrewd common sense, but he still winced at first sight of her boudoir. It had been assembled impeccably in green and cream— doubtless by one of her daughters—but subsequently "improved" with cushions, cloths, and ornaments in a rainbow of brash shades.

It was overwhelming, but it was so unabashedly in keeping with the lady's wishes that he was inclined to be charmed.

He came straight to the point. "I think it would be wise to invite Mr. Dunstable here for dinner, Lady Harby."

"Invite him here, Everdon? Why, pray? I have no time for the man."

"From what I hear, he is a rival for Lady Deirdre's hand."

She looked a little uneasy. "I don't deny, my lord, that Deirdre has an interest in that direction, and him in her. It will not be allowed to come to anything."

Everdon wondered what course Lady Harby had planned to prevent the marriage if the worst came to the worst. He had no doubt she had something in mind. She and Deirdre had much in common. "If that is the case," he said, "nothing is served by keeping them apart, and I would like to meet the man."

"Ah," she said, nodding. "Know your enemy, eh?"

"Not at all," he replied innocently. "It is just that I have an interest in mathematics."

Lady Harby snorted. "Have it as you wish, my lord. But I won't single out Mr. Dunstable. We'll have a small party in your honor—just dinner and an informal hop." She smiled. "I gather Dunstable don't dance, and has no conversation intelligible to lesser mortals."

Everdon returned her smile. "I see we understand each other perfectly."

Lady Harby fixed him with a look. "Do you intend to have her, then?"

Everdon took a pinch of snuff. "I consider us engaged to marry, Lady Harby."

"That's not what I asked. I reckon she's told you of that foolish agreement I made with her. If you cut loose, she'll end up with Dunstable."

"Lady Harby, I cannot possibly cut loose and still be considered a gentleman."

Lady Harby did not look particularly reassured.

She announced the plan for the evening entertainment at dinner, casually adding that Mr. Dunstable may as well receive an invitation.

Deirdre was startled, and immediately suspicious. After the meal when, as usual, Everdon joined the ladies ahead of the Stowe men, she asked, "Do I have you to thank for Howard's invitation, my lord?"

Deirdre had been sitting on a window seat near an open window that looked out onto a small courtyard full of roses, and he had joined her there. The wall beneath the window was covered by climbing roses, and the perfume filled the air.

"Now, why would you think I am to blame?" he asked.

"Blame?" Deirdre echoed warily. "Why blame?"

"An unfortunate choice of words. I confess, I expressed an interest in meeting the man, that is all."

"Why?"

"Why not? I have an interest in mathematics."

"I find that hard to believe, my lord."

He met her severe look with a pained one. "What

will I have to do to bring you to use my name, *querida*? Any of my names."

Why did a foreign language have such an effect on a lady's heart? Deirdre looked away and said, "Is that an endearment? Please don't. And as for your names, I cannot feel comfortable with that level of intimacy."

"Perhaps if I were to kiss you more often . . ."

She turned back sharply, then laughed. "I am beginning to get your measure, my lord. You delight in teasing. I will not dance to your tune anymore."

He said nothing, but leaned out of the window and plucked a spray of rambling roses—soft cream, blushed with pink. He carefully broke off the thorns, then said, "Stay still."

Somewhat to her surprise, Deirdre did as she was told, and stayed still as he tucked the roses into the fillet that held her hair on the top of her head. The feel of his fingers against her scalp was perhaps the most intimate sensation she had ever experienced, more so even than his kisses.

She looked up at his intent face. "I'm sure that looks very silly."

His eyes met hers, and only inches away. "Allow me to know about these things. It looks very well indeed." His hands were still raised, and she felt his fingers travel through her hair. "It is as delicate as silk."

"That's one way of describing it," she dismissed, seeking a brisk tone. "It's far too fine. It's impossible to do anything with it without hours of curling, and heavy applications of oil."

He caught a tendril and curled it around his finger. "I can think of any number of things to do with it, where such ministrations would be decidedly out of place."

Deirdre stared at him, dry-mouthed. "My lord . . ."

"Don."

"Don ... please don't ..."

"Don't what?"

Deirdre sidled away, so he had to release her hair. "You know perfectly well what. It is outrageous for you to be saying such things to a woman who is betrothed to another."

"But at the moment, you are betrothed to me."

"A mere fiction. It is unconscionable of you to trade on it."

"But I'm not," he said simply. "I've flirted like this with many women, none of them a future wife. If we really were betrothed, we would have progressed rather further, I think."

She looked at him in shock. "*What?* But you surely wouldn't ... I certainly wouldn't ..." She caught herself up. "Oh, you outrageous man! How do you make me speak of such things?"

His eyes laughed at her. "Do I make you? Then let me take you further." He captured her hand and kissed it, and would not let her flee. "My dear innocent, there is a world of sensuality between that kiss on the hand and the marriage bed, and the betrothal period is the ideal time to explore it. Otherwise, the marriage bed is likely to be somewhat of a shock. You should be traveling these paths with your mathematician."

He turned her hand and pressed a warm kiss into her sensitive palm.

Deirdre snatched her hand free, heart racing. "And probably would be," she said tartly, "if it were not for you."

But in the months since that unorthodox proposal, Howard had made no move to develop intimacy between them until today's clumsy kiss. They clearly did need practice.

The other men were coming into the room. "No," said Everdon softly. "If you had come back from London free to marry Howard, you would not be exploring gently. You would have rushed into it. I don't recommend it."

Deirdre rose, glad of an excuse to interrupt this discussion. "I hardly think your recommendations on marriage are of great value, my lord."

It was only when she was a few steps away that she realized he might take that as a comment on his failed marriage rather than his rakish life. She turned back, an apology on her lips.

His smile was wry. "There you may have a point, *mia*." He carried on, "The advice is sound all the same. Don't we learn best from our mistakes?"

Deirdre was achingly aware that she had hurt him. Before she could make amends, however, her brothers hailed Everdon to go off to play billiards, and she was glad when he agreed.

Then Henry said, "Why don't you come, Dee? I'd bet you could give even Everdon a match." He turned to the earl. "She's demmed good."

Everdon looked at her. "Are you, indeed? More surprises. Care to accept a challenge?"

Deirdre had been avoiding the billiards sessions, but she didn't see why Don Juan's presence should deny her all pleasures. "Very well, my lord."

As they walked into the hall, which housed the billiard table, he said, "What prize to the winner?"

Deirdre chose her favorite cue and blocked his next move. "I'm not playing for kisses," she said firmly.

"Very well. How about honesty?"

She turned. "What?"

He appeared suspiciously innocent. "The winner is allowed to ask one question and receive a completely honest answer."

On the surface it seemed innocuous—Deirdre did not think she had any dreadful secrets—but she distrusted the look in his eyes.

"Very well," she said. "But only as long as the question is not of an indelicate nature."

"So be it." His quick acceptance revived all her suspicions. What question did he have in mind?

He shrugged out of his tight-fitting jacket and set up the balls. Deirdre found his shirt-sleeved state, even though he retained both waistcoat and cravat, almost as stirring as she found Howard in that condition. Really, the fact that a lady only ever saw a gentleman completely and formally dressed had alarming consequences.

They tossed and he won the right to start. She soon saw he was very good. His action was smooth, he knew just where the balls should contact for greatest effect, and he was pretty good at planning ahead for future shots.

Not as good as she was, though. As soon as she had a turn, she quickly overtook his score. The turn changed a few more times, but she always pulled ahead. This wasn't surprising, for she was concentrating mightily. Deirdre had become quite certain that she did not want to have to answer Lord Everdon's question, whatever that proved to be.

When she executed her winning shot, however, he showed no particular chagrin. In fact, he applauded. "Bravo! Where did you learn to play so well?"

She knew she was flushed with victory. And relief. "I just practice a great deal. I find it a soothing discipline. I never went away to school—none of us girls did—so I've had plenty of opportunity to practice. My father and Rip taught me a little, but mostly I've taught myself."

"It's clearly a natural talent. Very well, ask your question."

Deirdre was taken aback. In her determination not to have to answer his question, she had given no thought as to what she would ask him. To her dismay, the only questions that came straight to mind were decidedly indelicate.

How many women had he made love to?

How old had he been when he first . . . ?

"I need time to consider," she said quickly. "Is it allowed that I claim my prize later?"

"Very well." His lips twitched. "*I* don't mind indelicate questions, you know . . ."

Deirdre quickly called upon her brothers to make up teams—she with Henry, Everdon with Rip. It proved to be an even balance, and the contest went on until the clock struck eleven and Lady Harby shooed them all off to bed.

Deirdre lay sleepless for many hours that night, wondering just what question to ask Lord Everdon.

And what question he had wanted to ask of her.

6

The next morning Deirdre took her mother's list and wrote out the invitations to the party. Then she hurried off to Foote's Cottage to deliver Howard's herself. She was fortunate, and caught him at a moment when he had attention to spare.

"At Missinger?" he said, reading the note. "But I thought your parents wouldn't let me cross the threshold."

"You know Mother doesn't approve of our plans, Howard. But I'm sure this is an acknowledgment that she will soon have to give in." Deirdre thought it best to leave Lord Everdon's machinations out of it.

Howard tapped the letter thoughtfully against his fingers. "Or that she believes she's won." He suddenly smiled at Deirdre in a way that reminded her surprisingly of Lord Everdon. "We'll have to make sure she realizes her mistake, won't we? You *are* very important to me, Deirdre."

He opened his arms, and Deirdre went into them, bursting with happiness. "Oh, Howard. I do love you."

"That's good," he said, and kissed her again.

This was much more like the time Everdon had kissed her by the barrow. There were strong arms around her, but this time she wasn't struggling. His mouth was more forceful.

More . . . sloppy . . .

Deirdre had to repress an urge to struggle. Where

95

was the magic of love? Nothing weakened her limbs, or made her want to surrender to more.

When he'd finished, she felt only a surge of relief.

Despite her efforts, he recognized her discomfort, but it did not upset him. He grinned. "What's the matter, little innocent? Am I too bold for you? You were the one wanting kisses."

"Yes, of course," she said, dragging up a bright smile. "Of course I want to be kissed by you, I mean. See how flustered you make me? It's just I am unused to such things."

"So I should hope." He turned her and sent her on her way with a playful but stinging slap on the behind. "Off you go. I have work to do."

Deirdre found herself out in the street in a daze, resisting the urge to rub her bottom. What on earth had come over Howard?

She headed back to Missinger, thinking that her world became stranger and stranger every day. Lord Everdon made her feel unlike herself, and now Howard, the fixed point of her life, was changing.

In their extraordinary conversation yesterday, Everdon had said she and Howard should be exploring sensuality in preparation for their marriage. Presumably this was what he meant: that it would take time to grow accustomed to each other, to come to enjoy kisses and ... and other things.

He had clearly been wise when he'd spoken against a hasty marriage. It was certain that she could not look forward to the marriage bed when she hadn't yet learned to enjoy Howard's kisses.

On the other hand, honesty compelled her to admit that she had quite liked Everdon's kisses from the first. What did that imply?

She tussled with this conundrum for quite some time, walking briskly along the path back toward Missinger.

It was, she decided at last, a simple matter of practice. Lord Everdon's skill came from misbegotten expertise, and therefore was nothing to be proud of. Howard's roughness doubtless came of inexperience, and was therefore proof of virtue. Both she and he would improve their skill in time.

She nodded as she walked. That explained it perfectly.

Perhaps she could make an aphorism of it, and distribute it to all young ladies.

Beware the man who kisses well.

She could embroider it on a banner to be hung at Almack's. She chuckled at the notion as she crossed the narrow bridge spanning the stream that divided the fields from the park.

"Happy again? Oh, lucky Howard."

Deirdre started. She looked down and saw Lord Everdon sitting by the stream below the bridge. Today the noontime heat had brought him to dispense with not just his jacket, but with waistcoat and cravat as well. Like Howard, he was in his shirt and breeches, and looked positively dangerous. He had even loosened his cuffs and rolled them up his muscular forearms.

"I am on my way back to the house," she said quickly.

He captured her eyes. "Come and keep me company." When she hesitated, he added, "Please, Deirdre."

Deirdre found herself walking down the gentle slope to sit by his side. At least she had the sense to leave three clear feet of grass between them.

"Now," he said, "tell me what makes you so happy today."

Deirdre knew it would be fatal to her composure to look at him. She concentrated on tossing daisies into the fast-flowing stream. "Just a general satisfaction with life."

"That must be very pleasant."

He sounded almost bitter. Deirdre sacrificed more daisies. "Are you not satisfied with life, my lord?"

"Not particularly. I want a bride, and it appears I do not have one."

She couldn't really believe he was hurt to lose her, and yet his words touched her heart. "I'm sorry. But the resolution is up to you, my lord. You have merely to disgrace yourself."

There was a movement. She glanced quickly sideways, but he had merely lain back, hands under head, to study the infinite blue of the sky. "I must confess, I am shirking my duty, Deirdre. I find myself liking your parents. I don't want to embarrass them by making them throw out a guest."

Once having looked, Deirdre found herself trapped. She hardly listened to his words for studying his body.

It looked even more impressive in the horizontal than in the vertical, and the tanned column of his throat, the vee of exposed muscular chest, were having a quite extraordinary effect on her nerves.

Then she absorbed what he had said and gathered her wits. "Are you going back on your word?" she demanded.

He glanced sideways, and even his dark eyes and lush lashes took on a new power at this angle. "No, *querida*. But I thought it might go easier if we all transferred to Everdon. Well, perhaps not your father—I know how it is with him. But your mother would accompany you, I'm sure."

She distrusted this move. She distrusted all of this, even as she felt him entangling her, just as a spider entangles a juicy fly. She inched a little farther away. "Why should we move? Are you trying to get me away from Howard?"

"Why should I do that?" he asked with apparent honesty. "He can come, too, if he wants."

"Howard? Come to your home?"

He rolled on his side, head supported on hand. "Why not? I have no objection to your courtship. The main advantage of moving this farce to Everdon Hall, Deirdre, is that I know all the available females there. I will be able to stage a spectacle to suit our requirements with no danger of hurting anyone, or creating more of a stir than we would wish. It will also mean that when you sever our connection in outrage, you will merely have to order your coach and depart while I stand gloomily by the door bewailing what I have lost. We need never meet again."

That caused a strange pang. "You are forgetting your mother," she pointed out.

It seemed he genuinely had. "I will try not to come between you. I'm sure you can find ways to meet without encountering me. But then, perhaps not. You will be married, won't you, and doubtless will not visit London again. I would have no objection to your visiting Everdon when I am absent if your Howard will permit it . . . But then there will soon be children . . . Marriage does tend to change things."

Deirdre was taken aback by this vision, even though it in no way departed from her expectations of her marriage. "Yes, of course marriage will change things," she said firmly. "It is not even clear where we will live. We will be at the cottage for a while, but Howard is talking of taking up the offer of a place at Cambridge. He does not want to teach, however."

Everdon appeared genuinely interested in her plans. "What he needs, surely, is a quiet place in which to think. The cottage seems ideal."

"It is, except that it is on the street, so he has to keep the windows shut. That is unhealthy. And it will be small when . . . if . . . " She broke off in confusion.

"When you have children," he supplied easily. "You will be able to buy something larger with your funds."

Her reaction was sharply defensive. "Howard is not marrying me for my money."

"I didn't say he was, Deirdre. But it will be pointless to stay in a cottage when you have half a dozen children."

Half a dozen children? Deirdre had thought in terms of one sweet, smiling cherub of a baby. Now she was prey to a vision of trying to keep the peace at Foote's Cottage with a horde of little ones underfoot. She'd seen enough crowded cottages to worry her.

"Lie back," he said softly.

"*What?*" Deirdre was jerked out of her concerns.

"I'm not suggesting anything dangerous. Don't you ever lie back and look at the sky?"

Deirdre did, when alone. Was he seriously suggesting that she lie down on the grass with him?

"Lie back and study the arch of heaven with me, Deirdre . . ."

He was.

Deirdre thought, however, that this was not an attempt at seduction, but simply what he proposed—a study of the sky.

Somewhat hesitantly she eased back onto the grassy slope, keeping the space between them. A quick sideways glance assured her that he wasn't planning an attack, but had rolled onto his back and was looking up at the sky. He'd put his hands to cushion his head, which made his shirt gape further open . . .

Deirdre hastily turned her own eyes upward.

The sun, fortunately, was behind them a little, and so there was little glare. There were no clouds today, and no trees just here, and so all she had to look at was infinite blue.

He quoted, "'I have learned to look on nature, not as in the hour of thoughtless youth; but hearing oftentimes the still, sad music of humanity.'"

"Wordsworth," she identified with pleasure, and made her own offering from the same poem, one composed on viewing the remains of Tintern Abbey. "'And I have felt a presence that disturbs me with the joy of elevated thoughts . . .' I'm afraid we have no such noble ruins here."

"There is Glastonbury not so far away."

"True. Do you know they say the young Jesus visited Glastonbury with Joseph of Arimathea? Some even say that the Holy Grail is to be found there."

"Is this the land of Arthur, then?"

"And of Guinevere."

"Who married a worthy man," he said softly, "but was carried off to destruction by the fevered power of romantic love . . ." After a moment, he carried on. "The stars are still up there, you know. They never go away, but we are blinded to them by the gaudy brilliance of the sun."

"But the moon sometimes prevails. Sometimes it can be seen in the daytime."

They lay there looking up at the sky and talking of wonders and little things. For a while they were free of social conventions and polite inhibitions. Then Deirdre looked sideways and found he was no longer looking upward. He was looking at her.

Her heart fluttered madly at the experience of being eye to eye with a man in the horizontal.

"Don't," she whispered.

"Don't what?"

"Look at me like that."

"Like what?"

"As if I were beautiful."

"You are."

"Don't mock me!" She would have scrambled up, but he rolled, and a strong arm and leg trapped her there. Caught in that heated prison, she stared at him, fearful yet excited.

"I do not mock," he said, his rich dark eyes flashing with anger. "Beauty is more than the shape of a jaw, the curve of a cheek. But if you want beauty," he said, and touched her cheek with heated softness, "your skin is beautiful. It has the luminous pallor of a pearl." A finger traced down her forehead, nose, and chin. "And your profile is delightful. I don't suppose you study your profile much. And your voice charms me. It sparkles with your spirit." That wandering finger traced her lips. "And your smile, *mi corazón*, your smile touches my soul."

His face was inches from hers, and his limbs pressed her down. This was more intimacy than Deirdre had expected in a lifetime.

She reached for a defense, any defense. "You can't pretend I blush prettily."

"No," he agreed with a smile, "but it still delights me to make you blush. As you are blushing now."

Her heart was doing a mad dance in her chest, and she felt hot from head to toe. "Oh dear," she said. "You're flirting with me, aren't you?"

His smile turned brilliant. "My dear Deirdre, don't you know?"

"No."

"Ignorance can be dangerous. Perhaps I should instruct you. This, little one, is rather more than flirtation. We are being very wicked."

At that, she made a tentative move to push him off, but her arms seemed to have become as weak as water. "Why are you being wicked with me? You don't really want to seduce me, I know you don't."

He eased his weight over her an alarming fraction further. "Don't I?"

"No," she said, but instead of a firm declaration, it came out as a squeak. "If you did, we'd have to marry."

His knuckles traced the secret underside of her jaw, and that brief touch sent excitement throughout her body. "I wouldn't mind marrying you, Deirdre Stowe."

"Oh dear."

"So if you decide that you and Howard would not suit, you mustn't hesitate to take me up on my offer."

That brought her back to reality. It reminded her that this was just a clever game he played, mostly fueled by boredom. She'd had a lifetime to learn she was not attractive to men, and to this man she was just a lottery ticket, no better, no worse, than any other.

Her strength came back and she pushed more effectively, though she failed to move him. "Get off me! I'm sure you'd like to save yourself the trouble of finding another ticket in the lottery of life, my lord, but I can't oblige."

He laughed, but she saw with amazement that she had made him blush. "My damn mother." Then he sobered and looked deep into her eyes. "No, Deirdre, you are by now far more than a lottery ticket to me."

Under that gaze, Deirdre weakened again. "I am going to marry Howard," she said firmly. "Let me up, please."

This time he obeyed and rose smoothly to his feet. He held out a hand to help her up, but she rose unaided. The farther she stayed away from Don Juan, the better.

He picked up his jacket and waistcoat but did not put them on. He climbed the bank beside her with them slung over his shoulder. "You will, of course, do just as you wish," he said calmly, as if those heated moments had never occurred. "I am looking forward to meeting Mr. Dunstable."

Deirdre looked back once at the slope, where flattened grass showed where they had lain. The grass would soon spring back and the evidence would be gone, but an impression of this interlude would linger in her heart.

She glanced uneasily at Don Juan. "You are not to be cruel to Howard."

"I am never cruel," he said, and they strolled back toward the house as if they were a conventional lady and gentleman, who would never dream of behaving in any way even remotely improper.

Thoroughly alarmed by the event, Deirdre disappeared off in the afternoon to visit Anna. Though Anna had not had the opportunity of going to London, she was much more worldly-wise than Deirdre, and much more practiced in the art of flirtation. Perhaps she would be able to make sense of what was happening. The visit to Starling Hall would also serve the excellent purpose of removing Deirdre from any occasion of further wickedness.

"I don't know how I came to permit it!" she declared to her friend, after having confessed all.

"Well, it wasn't so very terrible," said Anna, who was bright-eyed at the story. She giggled. "It wasn't even as if you broke your mother's law, and let him get his hands inside your clothing."

Deirdre stared into space. "But it felt as if I did," she whispered.

Anna shivered in delight. "I can't wait to meet him. If you truly don't want him, can I have him?"

This drew a laugh from Deirdre. "What a wonderful solution to everyone's problems! But I'm afraid nothing can come of it, Anna. Once he disgraces himself to set me free, your parents will not look kindly upon his suit."

Anna's bright blue eyes twinkled. "Unless he disgraced himself with me."

"Anna!"

Anna was rather pink, but she carried on. "It wouldn't have to be anything too outrageous. If you were to find us in a heated embrace, you'd be within your rights to return his ring, and he'd be obliged to marry me."

Deirdre didn't know why she felt such violent aversion to the plan, but she did. "I couldn't let you make such a sacrifice. And what about Arthur?"

She expected Anna to laugh at that, but her friend sobered. "There is that." She fiddled with her blue satin sash in untypical bashfulness. "There's no comparison in wealth or rank," she said, "but I rather think that in time, I may want to marry Arthur. It would be a pity to be already married to someone else."

"It certainly would," said Deirdre. "And hardly fair to Everdon. He's had one wife run off with another. He deserves to do better this time."

"Yes," said Anna thoughtfully.

"Anna, why are you looking at me like that?"

"Looking at you?" asked Anna innocently.

"*Looking* at me. I know that look. You're planning something. Oh, Anna! Have you thought of someone here with whom Everdon can disgrace himself? I really would prefer not to have to go to his home."

But Anna shook her head. "No, I haven't thought of anyone. Now, tell me who will be at the party ..." And no amount of urging could bring Anna to confess to plans, or secret thoughts.

Deirdre left Starling Hall an hour later, little wiser as to the ways of rakish men, and with no preventative techniques in her armory. She also now had to wonder what Anna might be up to. Hadn't it been Anna who had locked Deirdre in the buttery with John Ransom, because she thought it would promote a romance?

When Deirdre arrived home she disappeared into the safety of her boudoir, which was more precisely her sewing room. She needed the discipline of her art and the security of privacy.

She took out the watercolor sketches of her wild-flowers, and considered how best to portray them in silks. She knew the effect she wanted; that of wild-flowers scattered on a dark green velvet cloth. She wanted them to look real, almost as if they could be picked. She began to set stitches in a scrap of fabric, trying out different approaches and different threads . . .

A knock on the door made her glance at the clock. She had been here for two hours. Her mother must have sent up some tea. She called permission to enter and returned to her work.

It was the heaviness of the step that alerted her. She looked up sharply as Everdon put the tray down on a table.

"What are you doing?" she asked, alarmed.

He grinned. "Bringing your tea, milady. And mine. I encountered a maid sent on the mission, comman-deered the tray, requested an extra cup, and here I am." He lifted the china pot, just like a worthy ma-tron. "How do you take it?"

"A little milk only, thank you," said Deirdre weak-ly. Then she added, "Is this how you do it?"

"Do what?"

"Tangle women in knots. By always doing the unexpected?"

He considered it. "I don't think I've ever planned to tangle anyone in knots. Doing the unexpected makes sure people won't grow bored, but I do what I do because I want to." He brought over her tea, and a plate of cakes. "I invaded your sanctum for two reasons, Deirdre. One, because you are hiding from me here. Two, because I want to see your work." He placed her tea and cake on the small table by her el-bow, but then stayed to study her embroidery.

Deirdre wanted to shield it, unused to this atten-tion, and sure he would scoff. She had progressed to embroidering over little silk pads, to raise the petals and give them contours.

Everdon looked thoughtfully from the sketch to the velvet. "How real that looks. You have the colors exactly, and even the shape. I feel as if I should be able to pluck the bloom, able to smell the perfume of it. I beg you, don't make it into a cushion. No one will ever dare to lean their head on it."

He moved away to sit and drink his tea.

Deirdre glowed under his praise. Part of her was saying that he only flattered to manipulate her, but she had confidence in her work, and she knew this was good. She took a piece of seedy-cake and nibbled on it.

"Thank you," she said. "As to its use, I don't know what I shall do with it."

"Then give it to me as cloth, and I will decide."

When she looked at him in puzzlement, he said, "It was agreed, was it not, that this was to be my price for setting you free?"

Deirdre took a fortifying draft of tea. "Only if you behaved well in the meantime, my lord."

"And I haven't? In what way have I misbehaved?"

But Deirdre knew that talking about these things was extremely dangerous. She changed the subject. "Have you spoken to my parents about a visit to Everdon Park, my lord?"

"Yes, and your mother is completely agreeable." His lips twitched mischievously. "I confess, I neglected to tell her that I would be inviting Dunstable."

Deirdre almost choked on a mouthful of cake. "You can't do that!"

"I just have. It's amazing what one can do if one is shameless enough. Are you all right? Should I slap you on the back?"

Deirdre regained her breath and waved him away. "But she'll be most put out!"

"Put out enough to forbid you to marry me?" he asked hopefully.

Deirdre sobered at that. "I have come to realize that breaking this engagement is going to be unpleasant for you, Everdon. I'm very sorry. If I *could* act in your place, believe me, I would."

He considered her thoughtfully. "As to that, Deirdre, if you were to be found in Dunstable's bed, you would doubtless end up at the altar with him within the week."

Deirdre's mouth went dry and she wondered how she could have made such a foolish offer. He was correct, though. It was the obvious solution. How on earth was she going to bring herself to do such a thing? What would Howard have to say about it . . . ?

Everdon laughed. "I'm teasing, little one. I wouldn't expect you to act in such a way. For a hardened *roué* such as I, it is a mere nothing."

Deirdre's heart calmed, and she felt more kindly toward him than ever before, for she knew that despite his words, it would not be easy for him. Though his reputation was well known, she gathered that his affairs had always been conducted with discretion. She tried to imagine what anyone would feel—*roué* or not—at being caught in intimate disarray . . .

"By the way," he said, "if you don't object, your brothers are going to come along, too. There is a prizefight scheduled between the famous Molineux and a man named Carter. Everdon Park has the blessed fortune to be within a three-hour drive of Twistleton Gap, and so has become a Promised Land."

"No, of course I don't mind," said Deirdre, though she felt rather dazed. "Have you persuaded father to come, too?"

"No. Do you want me to?"

She raised her brows. "I'm tempted to set you the task, merely to see you go down to defeat, my lord. Only the sacred duty to marry off his daughters ever drags him away from his land."

He smiled and drained his cup. "But I would merely have to ask his advice on the management of my estates ..."

And Deirdre had to accept that would do the trick.

He gathered up the plates and cups, and assembled them neatly on the tray. Deirdre was astonished that he was so willing and able to play the maid, and that he was willing to go with so little teasing accomplished. "Are you leaving, Everdon?"

"It was my intent. Do you not wish me to?" He invested the question with layers of sultry meaning.

"Yes, of course I do. I want to return to my work."

"I could read to you as you sew. Byron? Mrs. Edgeworth? Wordsworth?"

She could not deny that the notion held some appeal. He had a lovely mellow voice, and the only thing she did not like about her work was the isolation. That was why she had loved her time with Lucetta, for they had been able to work and chat without interruption. Here at Missinger, however, Lady Harby took it for granted that Lady Everdon wanted to spend time with her, and Lucetta was too polite to disabuse her of the belief.

To encourage Everdon, however, would be perilous. "No, thank you, my lord. I just need peace and quiet to work."

He picked up the tray. "I will arrange a suitable room for you at Everdon Park, then. Until later, my dear."

He was gone. That had, all in all, been an unexceptionable visit. Why, then, did Deirdre feel as if it had pushed her world even more out of tilt?

* * *

The next day, as Deirdre dressed for the party, she reminded herself that she had always enjoyed these informal local affairs. They were quite different from the horrible London balls and soirées, for here she knew everyone, and most of her neighbors were delightful people. Even the few who were unpleasant, one had learned to put up with.

On this occasion, however, Deirdre found herself approaching it with anxiety.

Having been brought to the point, Lady Harby had gone all the way and invited Howard to dine. He would at last have the opportunity to win over her family, and if he could do that, Everdon would not have to put himself in an embarrassing situation.

In view of the importance of the event, Deirdre's nerves were in a terrible state. It *had* to go perfectly.

Lady Harby had insisted that Deirdre wear one of her new gowns, and so Deirdre and Agatha had spent the best part of the day stripping a pink and purple dress down to simplicity. To her surprise, the gown looked very well when all the trimming was removed, for the cut and material were excellent. Deirdre had embroidered some flowers on the bodice to cover marks left by the trimming, and Agatha had fashioned a sash of an ivory shawl.

The effect was as attractive as possible.

Deirdre hoped Howard would be as presentable.

As Agatha dressed her hair and worked up a few curls with the iron, Deirdre was tempted to rush down to Foote's Cottage to check that Howard was dressing appropriately, and that he had not forgotten the occasion entirely.

Everdon was also keyed up for the evening. Tonight he would meet his enemy. He chose a particularly fine embroidered waistcoat and a fawn cravat, wondering just what approach would be most effective.

"And how are you liking Missinger, Joseph?" he asked his valet.

"A very pleasant, well-run establishment, milord."

"I would imagine the staff think highly of Lady Harby."

"Indeed, though she does have her funny ways."

"And what of Lady Deirdre? Is she well liked?" He had said nothing specifically to his valet about his marriage plans, but it didn't take genius to work out why they were making this visit.

"Very well liked, milord." The valet cleared his throat. "I gather the older girls were inclined to be a bit sharpish with the staff, and the young men are a little wild, but no one has any word to say against Lady Deirdre. Always most considerate of the staff, she is."

"As I would expect." Everdon put the last touches to the arrangement of his neckcloth. "I gather Lady Deirdre has shown a certain interest in a young man. A Mr. Dunstable." He stood so Joseph could ease on his perfectly fitting jacket and caught an uneasy expression on the valet's face.

"I'm sure there's nothing to it, milord."

"But what is known of this man?"

Joseph smoothed the jacket, and brushed away a minute speck of fluff. "As to that, milord, he's considered to be an odd fish. He's a stranger, of course, and you know country people, but I gather he's had trouble finding a housekeeper on account of his finicky ways."

"Finicky?"

"I don't know any particulars, milord."

"Any other views? Any gossip?" Everdon kept the valet under surveillance in the mirror and saw the way his lips tightened.

"I don't hold with thirdhand tales, milord, but as

you have an interest, so to speak . . . it's said he visits a lady called Tess Biggelow. A widow."

Everdon turned. "And would this Tess perhaps be the local convenient?"

Joseph colored. "Yes, milord."

Everdon shrugged. "It would be absurd of me to be holding my nose at that, wouldn't it? You have the right of it, though. I have a particular interest in Lady Deirdre, so if you hear anything else that could have a bearing on the matter, I would appreciate your passing it on."

He turned and surveyed himself, considering the suitability of the pearl pin in his neckcloth. "Perhaps the diamond, Joseph. The large one."

Joseph brought the glittering pin, and Everdon fixed it carefully. A trifle gaudy for country wear, but . . .

No, it would not do. He changed it for the pearl.

At the door, he turned. "By the way, Joseph, Mr. Dunstable will be here tonight."

Joseph stared at the door after his master had left, considering that news. Very strange. He'd learned that Lady Deirdre's attachment to Mr. Dunstable was not approved by the family and that the young man was not received.

It was certainly true that the local people did not think much of him, but it was also true that village folk took time to warm to foreigners. He could be a worthy gentleman.

After all, though nothing was said directly in front of Joseph, it was clear the staff at Missinger had their doubts about the Earl of Everdon, too. They knew his reputation and couldn't believe he meant to deal honestly with Lady Deirdre, whom even the fondest of them admitted to be fusby-faced.

Joseph, however, had listened to people who had known Lady Deirdre from the cradle, and decided she was just what the earl needed. He was also watching his master's behavior, and was very hopeful, very hopeful indeed.

Tonight was the first time in years the earl had dithered about his appearance.

7

Deirdre was already in the drawing room with her family when Everdon entered. She was forcibly struck by how handsome he looked. She immediately prayed that Howard had taken some care over his dress so that he not be entirely outshone.

When Howard arrived—just after Sir Crosby and Lady Durham and their offspring, and just before the Misses Norbrooke—she breathed a sigh of relief. None of his clothes had come from a London tailor, but his dark pantaloons and jacket were unexceptionable; his hair had been trimmed, and brushed into a fashionable style; and his bow to her mother was perfect.

Deirdre saw her mother react to all this quite favorably. Lady Harby always had a soft spot for a handsome man. Just possibly, tonight would solve all their problems.

Howard looked rather lost, though, poor lamb. Deirdre went to greet him and drew him over to talk to her father.

"Mathematician, eh," said Lord Harby, who wasn't in the best of moods. He never was when forced into purely social occasions and deprived of his agricultural reading. "What use is it, eh?"

Howard wasn't thrown. "A clearer understanding of mathematical principles has proved useful in the past, my lord, and will in the future. Without geometry and trigonometry, most of our buildings would be impossible, and road building would still be a primitive art. The financial management of the nation demands a sophisticated knowledge of calculation, as does navigation and trade. Warfare would be hindered without the application of mathematics to artillery work."

Lord Harby perked up. "D'you say so? What good is it in agriculture, eh?"

"I am unfamiliar with the subject, my lord, but I am sure any number of calculations are necessary to plan crops and feeding patterns for cattle. It is quite possible that mathematical principles would enable better prediction of future production . . ."

Deirdre slipped away to help welcome more guests, ashamed of the fact that she was surprised that Howard could defend his discipline so well. He would have her father on his side in no time. Lord Harby always appreciated a man who knew his stuff, and one who could apply his science to agriculture was a sure winner. After all, her father had no particular attachment to Everdon. She hadn't seen them cozied up discussing silage and drainage.

Instead, Everdon, she noted, was showing his true colors as a social butterfly, and was surrounded by a crowd of guests. As the stranger in their midst, he was naturally of prime interest, and most knew of his reputation. The young women were visibly fascinated. If they were looking for the wicked Don Juan of Spanish literature, however, they would be disappointed. Everdon was behaving impeccably.

Deirdre well knew that if in the future any of these worthies should meet someone who made a disparaging remark about Don Juan, they would retort, "All a load of nonsense. Met the fellow at Missinger and found him a very tolerable sort. Thinks just as he ought on all subjects."

How confusing he could be.

Deirdre's sister, Eunice, Lady Ostry, had come to

the event with her husband. She, of course, was a typical Stowe—tall, handsome, and with lush blond hair. She, too, clearly admired Everdon. Deirdre saw them flirting, but it must have been in an unexceptionable manner, for her husband was standing by and didn't seem to mind.

On the other hand, Deirdre had always thought Lord Ostry a rather dim-witted man for all that he was a handsome six foot with a commanding air. One of the first things to appeal to Deirdre about Howard had been the power of his intellect.

Seeing Everdon raise Eunice's hand for a significant kiss, and her sister preen and blush, Deirdre had the alarming thought that the earl might choose *Eunice* with whom to create a scandal. That certainly would throw the fat in the fire. Didn't he realize Ostry was just the sort of blockhead who'd call him out?

She took three steps in their direction, intent on preventing disaster. Then she remembered that Everdon was going to stage the affair at his own home, and that he would be far too wise in these matters to risk disaster. She diverted her steps toward the Misses Norbrooke, two delightful old ladies.

She didn't know why she had developed this tendency to protect Don Juan; a more fruitless occupation was hard to imagine.

She was to go in to dinner on Everdon's arm—her mother insisted on it—and so he came to her as the meal was announced.

"Your swain has your father entranced," he remarked. "Is it possible that I will not have to exert myself?"

"I was wondering the same thing. But there is still Mother to consider. Father will rule her if he feels strongly enough, but he has to feel *very* strongly for it to be worth his while."

"I rather thought she mellowed a little toward Dunstable, so the cause may not be entirely lost. He's remarkably good-looking, by the way. I thought he'd be hunched and bespectacled."

Deirdre warmed to him. "He is, isn't he? Not that I let such things count with me . . ."

"Clearly. I'm even better-looking."

Deirdre looked up, prepared to argue, but decided it would be both foolish and ill founded. Simply on the basis of looks, Everdon could beat Howard all hollow.

As Everdon seated her, she said, "Howard will not take sufficient exercise or fresh air. I do try to encourage him."

Everdon took the seat beside her. "My dear Deirdre, don't carry his entire life on your shoulders. His course is his own, and the consequences also."

"But surely we should care for those we love. Am I to watch him harm himself and do nothing?"

A strange shadow passed over Everdon's face. "Perhaps not. But there is a limit to what we can do."

Then the green soup was being served and they could address their food.

The meal progressed smoothly, though Deirdre noted that Howard was improperly silent. He had been seated between the two Misses Norbrooke, which was doubtless a deliberate maneuver of her mother's as he could have little in common with them. Even so, he should be exerting himself. Everdon was managing to converse with Lady Durham, a rather silly and mean-spirited lady who could find something to carp at in everything.

Deirdre sighed. Howard was doubtless lost in calculations, poor lamb. If she were closer, she'd try to kick his shins.

Then she saw Miss Georgianna Norbrooke turn and start a purposeful conversation with Howard, and was grateful to the old lady. Even if Howard contributed little, it made him less conspicuous.

From her left, Everdon said, "I am sure he can manage a simple dinner without your focused gaze, Lady Deirdre." It had the edge of a rebuke, and Deirdre colored, aware that her behavior was almost as gauche as Howard's.

"He gets lost in his thoughts, that's all." She faced Everdon and summoned her social skills. "Did you have a good day's angling, my lord?"

"It was too hot for much, but it's always pleasant to pass time near the water."

She glanced at him, and his eyes trapped hers in an awareness of that magical interlude by the stream. Then, in a disastrous lull in the conversation, she heard Howard say, "Will you please stop chattering at me?"

She looked over to see Miss Georgianna turn away, red from the neck up. After a horrified hush, everyone plunged into talk to cover the moment, but Howard was left completely in peace.

Deirdre knew her face was as red as poor Miss Georgianna's. She wanted to hide under the table. A hand firmly covered hers. "You are not responsible for what he does," said Everdon.

"But . . ." Then she collected herself. "But I encouraged him to come tonight when I know he doesn't like chatter, and much prefers to be alone with his thoughts."

She risked another look at Howard. He seemed oblivious of any problem.

"Forgive me for mentioning it," said Everdon, "but doesn't his love of isolation make him a poor candidate for marriage?"

"For some, perhaps. I, however, am very quiet also, and generally much prefer to be left alone with my needlework." Deirdre addressed herself resolutely to her pork, praying that she wouldn't cry, and wishing this whole horrible evening were over.

As the time approached for the ladies to leave the table, Deirdre began to worry about what would happen to Howard. She was unsure what gentlemen did when left alone, other than drink more wine and take snuff.

Everyone was most fond of the Misses Norbrooke. Could it possibly come to a duel?

She leaned sideways toward Everdon and whispered, "Look after him, please."

His brows rose. "Wouldn't you rather I killed a dragon or two, my fair maiden?"

She just looked an appeal at him, and he shrugged. "I don't know if anyone will say anything, but I suspect he's pretty impervious to words. I'll make sure no one draws his cork." He took her hand under the cover of the table, and his thumb stroked her sensitive skin. Sensitive skin? She'd never thought of her small, capable hands as sensitive.

She looked at him warily, wondering what price he was going to exact for his assistance.

"Don't worry," he said, "I'll take care of everything."

In some way it seemed to encompass more than the matter of Howard's rudeness.

Then her mother rose, and Deirdre had to abandon Howard to his fate.

In the drawing room over tea, everyone fussed over Miss Georgianna, but the cause of the problem was not mentioned, or the reason for Howard being there. Deirdre, however, felt as if she wore a sign around her neck declaring her to be an accomplice to the crime.

Like Saint Peter, she would probably have denied any connection if challenged.

She went to sit safely by Lucetta, but the dowager's attention was soon claimed by another guest.

Then forthright Mrs. Treese, Anna's mother, took the seat on the other side of Deirdre.

"That Everdon seems a fine man," she said. "Can depend on a man like that to do the right thing."

"Do you think so?" said Deirdre, longing to raise his reputation as Don Juan. She could not do it, however, when sitting beside his mother.

In any case, she had to accept that Mrs. Treese was right. One could depend on Lord Everdon.

"Any gel would be lucky to get a man like that," said Mrs. Treese. Having made her point, she went on to discuss her younger son's military career now Napoleon was safely on Elba.

When Mrs. Treese left her side, Deirdre's sister took her place. "What a fool you are, Dee," Eunice said frankly. "I hear you're shilly-shallying over snapping up Everdon. I wish I'd had the chance."

"I'm not shilly-shallying at all," said Deirdre. "I'm definitely not going to marry him."

Eunice raised her finely curved brows. "Are you that much of an idiot? You'd give up the Earl of Everdon for that horrible scholar?"

Deirdre reddened. "He is not horrible. He just doesn't like these events."

"Then he shouldn't have come."

"I talked him into it." But Deirdre remembered that he hadn't been reluctant at all.

"Unwise to talk men into anything," said Eunice. "A word from me, Deirdre, don't think you can change a man. You have to take them as they are, and if you want Dunstable as he is, your wits have gone begging." She rose and drifted onward, an image of matronly wisdom, though she was only twenty-one.

Deirdre told herself that anyone would be cynical after two years of marriage to Lord Ostry, though in fact Eunice appeared to be happy with her choice.

Of course Deirdre wanted Howard just as he was.

She didn't want to change him in any significant way. She'd just encourage him to do a little more exercise, to go out and about a little more. She'd ensure he visited the barber regularly, and that his coats came from a better tailor. Once they were married, there'd be time for him to explain his work, then when she understood it, she might be able to help with all that tedious figuring. Then there would be more time for other things . . .

Deirdre hastily escaped her thoughts by joining Anna and the other young people. It was not really an escape. The talk was all of Everdon.

". . . so handsome," sighed Jenny Durham. "I could have swooned when he smiled at me."

"He touched my hand," said Anna, adding dramatically, "I felt it all the way to my heart!"

Deirdre rolled her eyes at her friend, knowing Anna was exaggerating in fun. She tried not to acknowledge that she had felt that way in very truth.

Jenny eyed Deirdre jealously. "Rumor says he's courting you, Deirdre."

"You know rumor," Deirdre responded. "Would you like more tea, Jenny?"

"I think he is," the girl persisted. Blond and pretty, she was used to being the local belle. She considered the homage of the eligible men hers by right. "I saw the way he was looking at you. Amazing really when . . ." Then she recalled her manners and did not say what she was thinking. "And I thought you were going to have to settle for that Dunstable man. Oh," she said with embarrassment, for she was not actually a cruel girl. "Yes, please, I would like more tea."

Deirdre summoned a maid to bring it.

Anna said, "It must be exciting to have such a man under your roof, Deirdre. He has such soulful eyes."

"Soulful," scoffed Arthur Kealey. "Makes him

sound like a dashed spaniel. I don't know why you girls will go on so."

"I doubt he has a soul at all," said Deirdre. "Be warned, Anna. It is his habit to flirt with any female who crosses his path. So guard yourself."

"If he pesters you, Anna," said Arthur stoutly, "you can depend on me to take care of it."

Deirdre and Anna shared a look at this absurdity, but Deirdre could see Anna was rather touched. Such devotion made her a little sad, though she couldn't think why.

Mary Kingsley giggled. "I don't mind if Everdon flirts with me."

"Mary," said Deirdre. "I thought you were pledged to Captain Hawksworth." How could she get them off this subject?

"So I am," said Mary unrepentantly, "but that doesn't bar a little harmless flirtation."

"I doubt Lord Everdon is harmless," said Deirdre darkly.

Her three female companions leaned forward. "Do tell."

Deirdre had never been so glad of anything in her life as the sudden entrance of the gentlemen. This appearance was rather speedy, and she suspected she had Everdon to thank. He gave her a knowing look and the trace of a wink. She noted that there seemed to be an invisible circle around Howard.

For a moment Deirdre was reluctant to go over to Howard, to associate with him before the company. She conquered the cowardice and crossed the room to where he stood. He smiled slightly, but seemed abstracted.

She couldn't just stand there like a sentry, and so she began to talk cheerfully of a sequence of light topics. He made no response. Did he even hear her? She stopped abruptly, afraid he would make matters worse by telling *her* to stop chattering, too.

He had done so before, she remembered. She had been making small talk as she'd been trained—for a silence is a terrible thing—and he'd said something like, "Do stop chattering so. I'm thinking."

She hadn't taken offense, for it seemed a reasonable request. She had found it something of a relief to be with someone without the need to talk, and she'd learned how to judge whether he was receptive to conversation or not.

But this was a different kind of occasion. Even her father acknowledged that one could not retreat into a private world when in company. Oh dear, what was she to do? She glanced over at Lord Everdon, but he was engaged in lively conversation.

Her silence finally seemed to penetrate Howard's thoughts. "What's the matter, Deirdre? Are you giving me funny looks, too? I suppose it's because of that old biddy. But really, she was going on and on about her cats. I have no interest in cats. I was devising what could be a most interesting development on Müller's mechanism. You see, if one were to consider . . . But you wouldn't understand."

No, Deirdre didn't understand, and about far more than geometry. "Howard," she said firmly, "Miss Norbrooke would consider it rude to leave you alone. It is polite at a dinner to talk to the people on both sides."

"I know that," he said brusquely. "But I can't be expected to abandon a significant insight for a discussion on fleas." Then Howard smiled, that quirky, boyish smile that tugged at her heart. "Was I very rude? Should I go and apologize? I could claim to have a toothache."

"Oh yes," Deirdre said in relief. "I'm sure that would be appreciated."

She watched surreptitiously as he went over and bowed to the frosty Misses Norbrooke. In moments the generous ladies were fluttering about him, doubtless offering their patent remedies. Word spread, and Lord Harby gruffly ordered a glass of brandy and ordered Howard to swill it around his mouth well before swallowing. Having followed orders, Howard announced that he was now free of pain, and thanked everyone for their kindness.

The company was now restored to happiness.

Except Deirdre. She thought it all terribly underhand.

Everdon appeared at her side. "A piece of advice," he murmured, his eyes dancing with amusement. "Always check their teeth before you buy."

"There's nothing wrong with his teeth," she snapped, before catching herself. "Oh, go away. This is all your fault."

"Now, how do you work that out, light of my life?"

Deirdre glowered at him.

He shook his head. "Next part of the course— accepting compliments. Anyone would think you'd never received any before."

"I haven't. Except about my embroidery, of course. Though few people really appreciate ... And my horsemanship ... I ... don't deserve—" She bit off that statement.

"At least you realize how absurd that is. You truly are the light of my life—for the moment, at least. I rise each day with enthusiasm, wondering what new wonders it will bring, and they all stem from you."

Deirdre grasped one phrase. "For the moment?"

"But of course. This can only be a fleeting paradise, alas. You are going to marry the man with the bad teeth. Mine are excellent." He stretched his lips in an exaggerated grin.

Deirdre cast a harried look around. "Do stop it!"

"Ah, I hear new arrivals. We will shortly progress to the dancing. I claim the first set."

Deirdre had little choice but to accept.

The dancing did not start for some time, for the new guests had to be welcomed and greeted by all, and gossip had to be exchanged. Within the hour, however, the music began and two sets were formed.

Deirdre was surprised to see Howard partnering Anna. Doubtless Lady Harby had dragooned him into it, for they were a little short of men, but she was surprised he had allowed himself to be dragooned.

He must be on his best behavior for her sake. That warmed her heart.

He was in the other set, so she could not watch him closely, but he appeared to dance quite well.

Everdon, as she knew, danced superbly, and she found the same magic occurring as had happened at the Ashby soirée—she danced well, too. She knew she was capable of it, but generally in public she felt so awkward that she became stiff and clumsy. She knew it was because deep inside she felt so plain as to be almost a figure of fun. Look how surprised Jenny Durham was that a man like Everdon would even consider her as a bride.

With surprise, Deirdre realized that the burden of being plain had been absent for days. This evening as she dressed, she had not once looked at herself in the mirror and wished her nose were more delicate, or her lips better defined. True, she had been fretting about Howard, but there was more to it than that.

As she joined arms with Everdon and spun around, her eyes met his, and he smiled as if he knew. " 'But oh, she dances such a way/ No sun upon an Easter day/Is half so fine a sight.' "

Then she was off dizzily into the arms of Sir Crosby.

As soon as the dance was over, Howard was at her side. "If I must dance, it will be with you, Deirdre. You dance surprisingly well."

She was thrilled that he'd noticed, but said, "Only one dance, though. Then you must partner the other ladies and make a good showing. I think you made a favorable impression on Father."

"He shows some sense for a farmer."

"A *farmer?*" she echoed.

"That appears to be his only occupation, so he is a farmer. He did show an interest in my work, but I could wish people appreciated knowledge in other than practical terms. If there were any justice, rich men would sponsor mathematics and science rather than useless painting and sculpture."

"Are not a great many people investing in the sciences and engineering?"

"In the hope of profit," he sneered. "They never get their noses out of the trough."

This was too much. He was as bitter as Lady Durham. "Really, Howard!" Deirdre exclaimed.

He started. She realized she simply did not speak to him that way. For a moment he looked angry, but then his boyish smile appeared. "Are you going to be cross with me, too?" he asked plaintively. "I thought you were different. I thought I could speak the truth with you, and not have to play silly games . . ."

The music started again, and Deirdre was saved from the need to reply, but not from the need to think. Was it her duty to listen to everything without debate, or was he being unreasonable? Of course he wasn't. She wouldn't want him to pretend with her.

As they took their places in the set, she smiled lovingly at him.

He smiled back and said, "It's a pity you aren't taller, for we don't suit very well as partners. I don't suppose you will grow now, though."

For some reason, Deirdre couldn't capture the lightness and ease she had found with Everdon, though he was almost as tall as Howard. Somehow her arm always seemed to be stretched, or their steps did not quite match. And yet Howard wasn't a bad dancer.

"You need more practice," he said at one point, and she had to agree.

When the dance was over, she slipped away, making an excuse of having broken a slipper ribbon, but in fact prey to a great weight of misery. She couldn't understand how everything was going so wrong.

In her room she wiped away some tears and bathed her eyes with cool water. All she needed was red, puffy eyes to add to her catalog of poor features.

She looked at herself in the long mirror and saw the creature she had known all her life—thin, flat-chested, with a long face, too large a nose, formless lips, and dull hair. Her elegant pink gown did not make matters worse, but no gown could make matters better.

Sometimes with Everdon she felt different—not beautiful, but attractive, charming, clever. It was just a foolish game he played, and she the fool to be taken in by it.

She turned away from the depressing vision.

As to her misery, it was her foolishness to have encouraged Howard to come to such an event. He might have made no protest, but she knew he had only come to please her. She had to accept that he would never move with ease through social waters, but such occasions would play little part in their married life. Their evenings would be spent at home, she working on new styles of embroidery, he working on his whatever-it-was geometry . . .

Deirdre had a sudden disturbing thought.

She had always considered Howard's intense application to his work as being part of this stage of his life, while he was working on whatever it was that would make him famous. But Eunice had a way of being right about things, and she must have more knowledge of men than Deirdre. What if Howard actually *liked* his present way of life—imperfect eggs excepted—and wanted it to continue forever?

For fifty years or so . . .

Deirdre hastily changed her slippers and returned to the party, where music and chatter would block out her thoughts. As soon as she walked through the door of the impromptu ballroom, her hands were seized by Everdon. "There you are. We are to give a demonstration of the waltz."

"What? But I've never danced it in public."

"Never?" he said. "Oh, poor Cinderella. But surely you know the steps."

He was pulling her farther into the room. She resisted. "Yes, Mama made me learn . . . but I only ever danced with Monsieur Decateur."

"Good enough. Ready?"

She was in his arms. The music started before she had a chance to think, never mind make a serious objection. She fell into a panic with no idea what to do.

"Step back," he said, and smiled at her with a carefree confidence in himself and her that would have made flying possible.

She stepped back and began to recall the moves, aided by his firm direction. They spun and swayed, alone together among others. She gazed into his eyes because then she could forget everything else—what she was doing, what people were thinking . . .

His eyes shone with approval. "I knew it. You waltz like a flower in the breeze."

She tried to remember her insight in her bedroom—that she was plain and awkward, and always would be. "That's because I'm so thin," she said.

"No, it's because you are lit from within. Smile for me, light of my life."

Deirdre smiled.

It was at that moment that Mark Juan Carlos Renfrew, Earl of Everdon, commonly know as Don Juan, decided he had to marry Deirdre Stowe. He'd felt the notion hovering for days, but had hoped it would fade, for he foresaw that it would bring him great trouble.

Now, however, the joy in her face would allow no escape. He knew, without doubt, that no other man would make her glow, especially not Howard Dunstable.

She would be quietly miserable with her mathematician, even if she never realized it. If she didn't marry Dunstable, she would almost certainly live her life as a quietly miserable spinster. Without someone to encourage her, she would cease twirling on the top of hills, or lying to look at invisible stars, or dancing the waltz like an apple blossom in the breeze.

Yes, he would have to marry her. The question was, how to bring her to agree.

Everdon knew it would be fatal to press her at this point. He didn't doubt that if he employed the full range of his arts, he could befuddle her, or even seduce her, but it would not solve his problem. If he inveigled her into bed, he could carry her to the altar on a wave of guilt, but he didn't care to contemplate the married life that would follow. Deirdre would not soon forgive that kind of scheming.

No, in the end she would have to see Dunstable for what he was, which would be easier to bring about at Everdon Park.

Their waltz ended to enthusiastic applause. Everdon focused one of his most powerful smiles on Deirdre and kissed both her hands with all the artistry at his command. He registered her flustered blush with satisfaction, then handed her without demur to young Kealey, who was most anxious to try the dance.

After a quick assessment, he bowed before Anna Treese, whom he judged to be the sort of girl who acted like a giggling ninny but who in fact had a very sensible head on her shoulders. Besides, he'd seen the looks she flashed at Arthur Kealey. Though the young man might not realize it, his fate was sealed.

She was not naturally a good dancer, but by the time the music stopped, she was beginning to get the idea.

"Goodness, Lord Everdon," said Anna, fanning herself. "That is not nearly as easy as you and Deirdre made it appear. I am not sure I care for it, either. It seems quite strange to have a man holding one so."

"I think in time ladies will become accustomed, Miss Treese. It is also the case that your feelings may change with your partner."

She endorsed his earlier assessment by flashing him a very shrewd look. "I suppose that could be true."

He gently took her fan and plied it for her. "The waltz offers delightful opportunities for flirtation."

"Really?" she said, with a teasing look. "But you hardly spoke to Deirdre, my lord."

"But then, I am hardly at the flirtation stage with Lady Deirdre, am I?"

"Perhaps you should be."

He raised a brow. "You mistake me, Miss Treese. Deirdre and I are beyond that."

She was not put out, but smiled. "Good."

Arthur Kealey appeared jealously at their side, and Everdon put the fan into his hands. The young man looked at it blankly. Anna bit her lip on a smile, and chose to look demure. Everdon left them to sort it out for themselves and went off to ask Mary Kingsley for a dance.

When it was over, Anna came over to him. "Deirdre's not here," she said.

He looked around and realized she was right.

"And nor is Dunstable," she added.

"Any idea where they might be?"

"No, but I did mention to him how strange it was that Deirdre dances beautifully with you, and badly with him. And how she smiles at you in a way quite differently to the way she smiles at him ..."

"Miss Treese, what are you up to?"

She unfurled her fan and plied it gently. "Just repaying you, my lord, for teaching Arthur a thing or two."

He shook his head. "I could pity Arthur."

She was taken aback. "Really?"

He smiled. "No. He's a very lucky young man."

He set off in search of Deirdre and Dunstable, wondering just what Anna's meddling had achieved.

He went into the hall and considered matters. He didn't think Deirdre and Dunstable were likely to be carried away by passion. If she was amenable to being seduced into marriage, however, it wouldn't do to let Dunstable get the jump on him.

The only innocent place for them to be was in the hall, and they were not there. A maid passed through with more lemonade for the dancers, but he did not inquire of her. Instead, he wandered, ears peeled.

He detected them at last in the morning room, with the door half-shut. Or half-open, thought Everdon, wondering if he should be optimistic or pessimistic. At the sound of his name, he did not hesitate to listen to their conversation.

"You can't be jealous of Everdon," Deirdre was saying. She sounded distressed.

"It seems to me to be entirely reasonable." Dunstable's voice was coldly accusatory. "He's an earl, and wealthy, thus more of your station in life. And after the way you danced with him, I cannot think you indifferent."

"It's just that he dances so well."

"Are you saying I do not? If our dance was less

successful, it was because you had all the grace of a bag of sticks."

Everdon's hand fisted, but he controlled the urge to go in and knock the oaf out. That would not help Deirdre.

"I know that, Howard," she said quietly. "But I care nothing for Everdon. I will not dance with him again."

"Very well," said Dunstable. Then his tone softened. "I am only thinking of you, Deirdre. If he's pretending to care for you, it can only be for your dowry. A man like that wouldn't really be interested in a dab like you, and he'd never stay faithful. Don't forget he's called Don Juan."

"I don't forget that, Howard." Deirdre's voice was scarcely more than a whisper.

Everdon wanted to horsewhip the insensitive cad, but he also wanted to throttle Deirdre for putting up with such treatment. She was spirited enough with him. What hold did Dunstable have over her? Love? He couldn't believe love led to this kind of . . . slavery.

"There, there." Everdon guessed that Dunstable had taken Deirdre in his arms, and he was even more tempted to interrupt, but he needed to understand what was going on here if he was to rescue her. "I'm sorry for upsetting you, but you know how important you are to me, Deirdre. I don't know how I'd get by without you."

She chuckled. "Nor do I, love. You'd be skin and bone in weeks."

"Have you looked for a new housekeeper?"

"Oh, I'm sorry. I've been so busy . . ."

"Running around with Everdon."

"I am supposed to be engaged to marry him, Howard," Deirdre said apologetically. "But I am sorry. I'll look into it tomorrow . . ."

Everdon gritted his teeth. Where was her backbone? Where was the woman who'd threatened to knock his block off?

"The sooner your engagement is over, the better. When will he arrange it?"

"He wants us all to visit Everdon Park. He says it will be easier to arrange there."

"What? He's trying to separate us."

"Why would he do that, Howard? As you say, he has no real interest in me. Besides, he says he will invite you, too."

There was a silence. "How strange."

At the note in his rival's voice, Everdon reminded himself that the man was no fool. He might well be lacking in social graces, and even in kindness, but when it came to putting two and two together, a mathematician would surely be able to make four.

Deirdre spoke softly, pleadingly. "He knows you are important to my happiness, darling, and he is a kind man in his own way. You will come, won't you? I couldn't bear to be weeks without you again."

"I don't see why it should take weeks," Dunstable said peevishly. "All he has to do is to be found in a woman's bed. He could drag one of those giggling chits out of the ballroom and get it done."

"Howard! He'd never seduce an innocent. And besides, then he'd have to marry her, which would be no part of his plans."

"Serve him right," said Dunstable. "Oh, very well. But I *will* come, and I'll keep an eye on him and you. You women are too foolish where such a man's involved. I wouldn't be surprised to find he's decided to taste you before he lets you go, and you'd be fool enough to let him."

"Howard!"

Everdon waited for the sound of a block being knocked off. When it didn't come, he sighed and pushed open the door.

He coughed.

Dunstable and Deirdre sprang apart. Deirdre looked rather relieved, which didn't surprise Everdon. He had not thought that kiss a masterly example of tenderness. Aggressive possession, more like.

"What the devil do you want?" asked Dunstable.

Everdon toyed with the notion of letting Dunstable pick a fight—he'd enjoy drawing his cork—but discarded it. Deirdre would see her hero as the victim. "People are wondering where Lady Deirdre is," he said smoothly. "We don't want to cause talk."

Dunstable looked as if he would argue, but Deirdre laid a pleading hand on his arm. "Please, Howard."

Everdon said, "Why don't you go back, Dunstable? We'll be along in a moment. If we all return together, it will look as if I'm shepherding back the erring sheep."

Dunstable flashed him a cold look. "Don't think you can play your games with Deirdre, my lord. I've warned her about you."

"I'm sure Lady Deirdre is far too honest and intelligent to fall prey to such as I, Mr. Dunstable."

"Intelligent? Good Lord, she's a practical little thing, but she don't even know algebra."

Everdon almost began to feel sorry for the fool. "I don't suppose you know bullion work from couching, Mr. Dunstable, or how to get rust stains out of linen."

Dunstable stared at him blankly. "What the devil has that to do with anything? It's my opinion you're more than half-mad." He flashed a look at Deirdre. "I'll leave this room, but if I'm to be denied the only pleasure of the evening, I'm for home. I could not bear more of that inane company, and I want to get my thoughts down before they're lost in a welter of feline fleas. Make sure you don't stay here long with him."

With this terse command, he stalked out of the room.

When they were alone, Deirdre made no move to obey Howard and rush back to the dancing. She looked away toward the empty fireplace, and Everdon suspected she was fighting tears. She was certainly distressed, and well aware that her beloved had not shown well. He wondered what made a woman endure a man like that for a moment, never mind a lifetime.

He took a thoughtful pinch of snuff, and asked, "Would you like some?"

She turned to face him. "What?" Her eyes were a little damp.

"Snuff," he said, extending his mother-of-pearl box.

A bemused smile flickered on her face. "Ladies don't take snuff these days."

"Very wise. It's a vile habit, and becomes compulsive in times of stress." But he still extended the box to her.

She looked at the powder. "What do I do?"

"Take a little pinch, hold it in your nostril, and sniff."

With an uncertain glance at him, she followed his instructions. She sniffed, then sneezed, then said, "Good heavens! Oh, my eyes are watering . . ." After a moment, she added, "I feel as if my head is expanding."

He smiled and put the box away. "More space for rational thought, perhaps. We should go back in case your devoted admirer is hovering. I don't want to duel him. It would probably be logarithmic tables at twenty paces and he'd beat me hollow."

She chuckled and blew her nose, then grimaced at the brown stain on the handkerchief. "I don't think I shall take to snuff, my lord."

"Can I not lead you into even a minor vice?" he asked, and gained an honest laugh.

"I fear not. I am destined for a life of sober industry."

"Caring for Howard Dunstable." He kept his tone very neutral.

"Yes," she said, equally blandly. She came over to his side and looked up pleadingly. "He is brilliant. Now you've met him, you do see, don't you?"

He placed her hand on his arm, and they turned to leave the room. "Oh yes, Deirdre. Now I've met him, I do indeed see."

Everdon was summoned to his mother's room before retiring. She was already in bed and he perched next to her.

"You cannot allow Deirdre to marry that man, Marco," she said forthrightly.

"Is not that what I said when we discussed this last?"

"I had not met him then."

"But, *Madrecita*, can you blame the man for not being interested in fleas?"

"What?"

He described what had occurred in the morning room. "Now, you tell me, what makes Deirdre put up with the man?"

Lucetta sighed. "Oh dear. It is hard to explain, but it happens. I think it is perhaps that once a woman commits herself, it is hard for her to abandon someone."

"Not in my experience," he said bleakly.

She covered his hand. "Genie was an unusual woman, dear. Deirdre is nothing like her."

"I know that. So how do I make her prove unfaithful to the man she has pledged to love forever?"

Lucetta frowned over it. "I am not sure. The best

course, if it is possible, might be to make him reject her."

Everdon shook his head. "That would hurt her terribly. I want her to knock his block off."

"What?"

"Never mind. There must be some other way."

"Then try to find it. But if she believes he loves and needs her, she will stay with him despite his petty cruelties."

"It makes no sense."

Lucetta smiled sadly. "It does, in a way, to a woman. And think of it another way, Marco. Would you forgive her for a cruelty? And would you expect her to forgive you? Where should it stop?"

Everdon wandered off to his own room, thoughtfully contemplating the fact that some of the qualities he most admired about Deirdre Stowe—her fidelity and determination—were what bound her to a man who did not appreciate her at all. If the only way to free her was to destroy those qualities, could he do it?

Should he do it?

He supposed he could in some way let her know that her Howard used a whore, but if that ruled out marriage, he was a dead duck.

He poured and drained a large glass of brandy, plagued by the fact that for the first time in his adult life, he was at a loss as to how to handle a woman. Even if he made Deirdre fall passionately in love with him, there was no guarantee that she'd abandon Howard; nor, as his mother pointed out, would he want it any other way.

He valued fidelity above all things.

8

They traveled to Everdon Park in two coaches and two curricles. Henry, Rip, Everdon, and Howard shared the curricles, though Howard did not drive. Lady Harby, the dowager, and Deirdre traveled in one chariot; the personal servants traveled in and on the other. A number of Everdon's servants attended on horseback to smooth their way.

The journey took two days, but under Everdon's organization, it was without incident. The best horses were always brought out at a stage—previously selected by his men. Their stopping places were always prepared for them; and the Bear in Reading, where they spent the night, was virtually overhauled for their comfort. Feather pillows and Persian rugs had been sent from Everdon Park, along with a special firm mattress for the dowager, for she found a soft one bothered her hip.

The meal was superb, though whether that was extraordinary or not, Deirdre had no way of knowing.

After the meal Lady Harby and the dowager took seats in the garden to chat in the evening sun, while Henry and Rip sauntered off to explore the delights of the town.

Deirdre was inclined to join the older ladies, but she was not at all sure she should leave Howard alone with Everdon.

Howard had as usual been abstracted throughout the meal. Now he suddenly addressed a maid who was clearing the last of the meal. "Is Sonning Eye near here, girl?"

"Aye, sir. It's but a mile north."

Howard turned to Deirdre and Everdon. "Quentin Briarly lives there. I'd very much like to meet him. He wrote an interesting paper on the Leibniz-Newton controversy. I think I'll walk out there."

"Excellent idea," said Everdon genially. "And these long nights, you won't have to hurry back."

"True."

To Deirdre's astonishment, Howard set off without apparent concern that he was leaving his future wife to the tender mercies of a rake—a rake of whom he had been jealous quite recently.

Deirdre definitely decided she wanted to join the older ladies, and rose to do so. Everdon caught her hand, staying her. "Do you really want to sit again, after sitting all day? Why not come for a walk with me."

Deirdre hesitated. She was strongly tempted, but by the chance to stretch her legs, not the company.

Everdon met her eyes. "I give you my word, Deirdre. No kisses, no flirtation, nothing to disturb you at all."

"Are you capable of it, my lord?" she asked with an edge, for even then his thumb was making tiny circles on the back of her hand. She allowed herself to be persuaded, however, and they set out to stroll about the town.

It was not a particularly remarkable town, and being on the Bath road, the High Street was very busy. They soon turned away from the thoroughfare to take a path that ran beside the River Kennet.

There it was more peaceful, more suitable for a summer evening stroll. Ducks paddled and bobbed in the river, and feeding fish made little circles in the glassy smoothness. Insects buzzed among wildflowers, and birds chirped and sang in the heavy trees.

They walked in companionable silence for a while, then Everdon said, "You need insects."

"I beg your pardon?"

He gestured to drift of wild phlox, busily worked by bees. "Your wildflowers need insects on them."

She focused and saw that he was correct. Whoever saw wildflowers without insects about somewhere? She cast him a teasing look. "Greenfly, perhaps?"

He didn't rise to the bait. "If it pleases the artist in you."

"It's your cloth."

"I'll hold you to that."

Deirdre looked back, studying the scene. She soon saw that in addition to the fat bees with the full yellow leg-sacks, there were smaller ones—or perhaps they were wasps. There were also ladybirds, and some little flies with bronze iridescent wings.

"Now, how would I get that effect?" she wondered, and crouched down to study them closer. She disturbed a grasshopper, and it leapt, bright green, out of her way.

"Poke your nose any closer," said Everdon in amusement, "and one of those bees will think you're a blossom and mine you for nectar."

She laughed, and let him help her to her feet. "Not very likely."

He steadied her with hands on her shoulders. "Very likely indeed. I'd like to mine you for nectar. May I break my word?"

The look in his eyes made Deirdre want to say yes, but she shook her head.

"Shame." He sighed and let her go. "I must beware in future of foolish promises." He tucked her hand back in his arm, and they strolled on.

To cover the moment, Deirdre said, "You're right about the insects. I must look for a book on them, for I cannot collect them."

"Yes, you can. One nets them, then pins them into a box to be studied at leisure."

She shuddered. "I couldn't do that."

"Consider that a blood sport, do you?"

She met his eyes. "Tease as you will, Lord Everdon, but if I can't swat wasps, I certainly couldn't stick a pin through a ladybird."

"I suppose not. I believe we have a collection of insects at home. Work of an uncle of mine. You could have that, if your stomach is up to it."

Her smile was rueful. "Is it very foolish? I confess I wouldn't mind if the pinning is long since done."

"I enjoy pork, but I leave the slaughtering to others."

They turned to retrace their steps, but halted to watch a kingfisher dive in a flash of blue, then emerge triumphant with a fish flapping desperately in its beak.

"It's a cruel world, isn't it?" said Deirdre.

"So there's no reason to look for extra trouble."

Deirdre took a deep breath and faced him. "Does that refer to Howard?"

Everdon was very serious. "Yes. He won't make you happy, Deirdre."

"You must allow me to be the judge of that."

"I cannot do anything else, but I'm laying my cards on the table. I don't think he's the right man for you, and I hope you will come to see it. Then you will marry me."

Deirdre wished he weren't doing this. This stroll had been a halcyon time, but now he was scarring it. "If I came to see it as you wish, I still would have other options than marriage to you."

"Am I so objectionable?" She could swear she saw hurt in his face. Don Juan, hurt by her? Surely not. All the same, she felt compelled to kindly honesty.

She looked away and softly said, "No, you are not objectionable, Everdon."

"So if you decided not to marry Dunstable, you would marry me?"

It was an honest question and deserved an honest answer. Deirdre stood in thoughtful silence, looking over the river to the meadow beyond, trying to imagine marriage to this man.

"I might," she admitted. Then she turned and added more firmly, "But don't think you can play tricks on me. I intend to marry Howard, so the question will not arise. You may as well set about choosing another bride immediately. After all, it can make little difference to you."

"Can it not? But I do want to marry you, Deirdre."

"Not to the exclusion of all others."

He considered it carefully. "I suppose not, but that's because I haven't met all others. Of the women I have met, I think you would suit me best."

Breathing was becoming more and more difficult. "Why?"

"Begging for compliments?"

She refused to smile. "You know me better than that, Everdon. I am begging for reasons."

She expected a quick and facile response, but he pondered it, frowning slightly.

"I enjoy being with you, Deirdre," he said at last. "In silence and in speech, apart or in one another's arms. Can you think of a better reason for marriage? Looks will change with time, passion cannot last a lifetime, but I believe I will always enjoy your company and your discourse."

Deirdre stared at him. "Goodness."

"I don't know why it should surprise you. Many people like you. I like you. I don't think Howard Dunstable does."

Deirdre was thumped back into harsh reality. "That's a terrible thing to say!"

"It's the truth. I'd tell you to ask him, but he'd be bound to assure you that he does like you—not from dishonesty, but because anyone would. But look to his actions. He doesn't behave as if he likes you at all."

Deirdre turned and started briskly back to the inn. "You don't know anything about the way he behaves. Just because he's not always trying to kiss me . . ."

He kept pace with her, damn him. "That has nothing to do with it. I'm not talking about lust, Deirdre, but liking. When has he ever sought to spend time with you?"

Never! echoed in Deirdre's head like a tolling bell. She clapped her hands over her ears. "Stop it! Stop it! Stop it!"

Everdon grabbed her and pulled her against his chest. She struggled feebly, both against his hold and against tears. "Oh, Deirdre, I'm sorry. Don't cry. I won't say any more."

Deirdre gritted her teeth to conquer the tears, but nothing could conquer the words he had planted in her head. She pushed, and he let her go. She turned away, rubbing at her eyes. "You're horribly cruel."

"I don't want to see you unhappy."

"Howard won't make me unhappy." It was like a litany, a mindless declaration of faith.

The silence stretched so that it rasped at her nerves. What was he doing? How did he look? She turned. He was very sober and concerned.

He sighed, took her hand, and kissed it. "Just be sure of your happiness, Deirdre, for my sake."

Then he placed her hand on his arm and they continued their walk, but did not speak again all the way to the inn.

Deirdre desperately wanted to talk to Howard, to investigate all these doubts, and to erase them, but he was still out. Rip and Henry were playing piquet, and she didn't want their jovial company anyway. Both her mother and Lucetta had retired. She certainly didn't want to speak to her mother about this, and she suspected Lucetta wanted her to marry Everdon.

She retreated to her own room and prepared for bed, then she dismissed Agatha and sat by an open window to face her problems.

Why on earth was Everdon attacking her like this? In another man, she could suspect the sort of mischief-making that comes of boredom, but she knew Everdon wasn't that sort of man. She had to suppose that it was simple misunderstanding. He clearly didn't like Howard, and could not imagine how anyone else could. He truly believed that Howard would make her unhappy, and being of a kindly disposition, he wanted to help. It was ridiculous, but that must be it.

She suspected, however, that Everdon would drag his heels about setting her free until he changed his mind. She would just have to work at convincing him that she and Howard were ideally suited. At Everdon Park, where they would all be living in the same house, that should be possible.

After all, Everdon was basing his doubts on that one disastrous evening at Missinger. That wasn't the real Howard, as he would see.

However, as Deirdre settled into bed, the traitorous thought crept into her mind that it *would* be very pleasant if Howard just once waylaid her as Everdon did, seemingly just for the pleasure of her company. Then she fought it away, furious with the earl for planting these corroding notions in her head.

Everdon watched Dierdre flee and wondered whether his actions were fair, or even effective. He'd never been involved in such a case before, and had no notion of how to go on. To him, Deirdre appeared to be intelligent, spirited, and generally wise. Why could she not apply those qualities to her own situation?

Dunstable had been Everdon's traveling companion for part of the day, and he had come to know him a little. The younger man had been an unexceptionable companion—if one did not care for conversation. Everdon had been determined to draw him out, however.

He had known that a question about mathematics would elicit some response, but he had no particular desire for a lecture, and so he raised the subject of Cambridge.

"You were there, too, my lord?" Dunstable asked.

"Yes. Pembroke."

"King's," said Dunstable, giving the name of his college. "I don't suppose our times overlapped."

"No, I left in 1805."

"Then we didn't miss by a great deal. I went up in 1807."

Everdon flicked him a glance. "Are you older than you look?"

"I don't think so. I went up when I was fifteen."

Everdon concentrated on steering the curricle at speed around a tricky corner. He wished Dunstable would prove to be a posturing nonentity, but he suspected nothing could be further from the truth. The man was almost certainly brilliant, but he still was no husband for Deirdre, perhaps for any woman.

"And when did you take your degree?"

"I took my first degree in 1811. I could have been speedier, but there were many intriguing sideways. I was not sure at that time what direction would suit me best."

"But you have now decided on pure mathematics. Is that the correct phrase?"

"It's as good as anything. I pursue knowledge for its own sake. I am wondering, my lord, if you have thought of being a patron of the sciences."

Everdon almost laughed. No wonder Dunstable had deigned to converse. Was he incredibly brash? No, just oblivious to any subtle nuance outside of his own narrow vision.

"A patron of the sciences?" Everdon mused. "Of you, sir? But was it not then a little unwise to take me to task over Lady Deirdre?"

Dunstable looked at him, blankly. "What has one thing to do with the other?"

"If you have annoyed me," said Everdon plainly, "then I am unlikely to provide you with financial support."

"Well," said Dunstable severely, "if you wish to reduce matters to that petty level, there is no more to be said. I will not grovel."

"I don't think I asked for that. And what of Deirdre in all this?"

It seemed as if Dunstable would not reply, but then he said, "It is Deirdre I am thinking of. I am well aware of the difference in our rank and fortune. I would prefer to be able to keep her in a comfortable manner."

Despite the words, Everdon received the distinct impression that Deirdre had not been in the man's mind at all until Everdon had raised the subject. Dunstable wanted extra income so as to be able to pursue his work without distraction. Deirdre was more likely a means to comfort, not someone to be made comfortable.

However, Everdon suspected that trying to persuade Dunstable of the selfishness of his actions would be like trying to persuade a fox that it shouldn't eat chickens.

Everdon then asked some mathematical questions—in his role as potential patron—and eventually decided he was correct in all respects. Dunstable was quite incapable of considering anyone else's wishes or feelings. He was also brilliant, and very likely to take humanity forward in knowledge.

In fact, thought Everdon that night as he went to bed, he would probably be doing humanity a service by preventing Dunstable from cluttering up his life with a wife and children.

Deirdre faced the next day with trepidation, but that turned out to be needless. Everdon staged no more assaults, and Howard had so enjoyed his scholarly visit that he was almost jovial. The weather held fine, and they made good speed toward Everdon's Northamptonshire home.

At the last stage, where they stopped for light refreshments, Rip challenged Everdon to a race.

Everdon raised his brows. "You young creatures. After a day on the road, you're up for this?"

"Pooh. What's a few hours driving? You're a notable whip, I know that, Everdon, but I reckon I can beat you."

Everdon gave a lazy smile. "Indeed? How can I resist? So be it."

But Howard said, "I have no intention of risking death. I will ride in the coach."

"You can't," protested Rip. "Henry would have to join you to make the weight even, and there's not enough room."

"And I'm dashed well *not* sitting out," said Henry. "In fact, I want to take a turn with the ribbons."

"Stubble it, whelp," said his brother. "Not in a race. Dunstable, you'll have to come."

"I'd rather walk," said Howard simply and irrevocably.

It appeared to be an impasse, and Rip and Henry glowered at Howard in a way that would have shriveled a lesser man.

Everdon looked at Deirdre. "What about you? Are you willing to risk death?"

"Travel in your curricle?" she asked, wide-eyed. Her glance flickered between her mother and Howard, gauging their reaction. Lady Harby frowned slightly, but seemed unwilling to object to anything that threw Everdon and her daughter together. The matter seemed to be passing over Howard's head entirely.

Deirdre didn't know what to do. Common sense told her that she should avoid Everdon, and that curricle racing was dangerous. Her soul wanted to do it for the sheer excitement. At least one fear was clearly foolish; Everdon would have no time for flirtation or even innuendo while driving to an inch.

Her instinct told her he would keep her safe.

"Very well," she said.

There was a bit of further debate about weight differences, but Everdon solved this by having a few bags moved to the boot of his curricle. All was set.

As everyone went out to the vehicles, Howard seemed to finally realize what was toward. He frowned slightly, but all he said was, "You are being remarkably foolish, Deirdre."

Deirdre waited for more, but he just walked away to take her seat in the carriage. If only he had taken her in his arms and said, "You will do such a foolish thing over my dead body!"

She sighed and took her seat in Everdon's curricle, prepared to hang on for dear life.

"Don't worry," said Everdon, "I'll let your brother beat us hollow before I endanger you. One learns at some point what is important in life and what is not."

"And winning isn't important, my lord? Shame on you. *I* want us to win."

His eyes sparkled. "Then we will. But with some precautions." He called over to Rip, and it was soon arranged that Rip and Henry would leave ten minutes ahead of Everdon. The victory would be based on time.

"This way," said Everdon, as the brothers disappeared in a swirl of dust, "we at least are not jockeying for position on the road."

"But how will we know if we're gaining or not?" Deirdre was almost bouncing with the desire to be off in pursuit.

He had his watch out, and was keeping track of the time. "We won't. I'll just drive my damnedest. Calm down, *mi corazón*, or I'll think I should harness *you* up. Do you drive?"

"Yes. Mostly the gig, though I have driven a curricle."

He passed her the reins. "Walk them, then, while we wait for the time to be up."

Somewhat nervously, Deirdre guided the horses down the road, then turned them back. It was silly to be nervous of such a routine matter, so she flicked them up to a trot. They were Everdon's own horses, sent here to await him, as were the pair Rip had. They were fine cattle, and she relished the feeling of power at the end of the reins.

Everdon clicked his watch shut. "Right. Off you go."

"*What?*"

"Go." He took the whip and urged the horses up to moderate speed. Deirdre concentrated on managing them, though in fact, the road presented little challenge just here, being smooth and straight.

"You're mad!" she cried, but grinning all the same. "We'll never win with me driving."

"Yes, we will." He set the whip back in her hand. "I'll take over in a while—your arms won't take this for eight miles—but you're doing marvelously. Just watch out ahead. There's a hidden dip."

Deirdre steadied the team and felt her stomach lurch as they went down, then up. "Criminy! I'll go odds Rip and Henry almost tipped out there." She urged the team to speed again.

She spared a glance at her companion, and saw him lounging back in a way that spoke eloquently of confidence in her. She couldn't imagine who else in the world would trust her with this team, though in fact, years of managing Charlemagne meant she was not nearly as fragile as she appeared.

The wind of their speed was dragging at her bonnet, and the dry road was blossoming dust, but Deirdre didn't have a care in the world. She let the horses have their heads, and took a gentle corner like a bird in flight.

She let out a whoop of pure delight, then had trouble as the horses tried to flee this howling monster behind them. She regained control, but wasn't regretful when Everdon said, "Better let me have them now." She steadied them down to a slow pace, and passed the reins and whip over.

He brought them up to speed again and set to catching the challengers.

He was a marvelous driver. The horses seemed to be an extension of him, and his eye for the road was impeccable. Of course, he must know this road well, but that wouldn't help him anticipate the branch that had fallen on one side, or the sudden appearance of a trio of runaway piglets.

Deirdre relaxed to enjoying the thrilling speed, straining her eyes ahead for any sign of Rip. "I can't see them. They're still ahead!"

"Of course they are. I don't hope to catch them before the park gates. The driveway is a mile, and very open. I hope we'll overtake them there. If not, I promise we'll wipe out most of their lead."

He was almost exactly correct. In fact, they came up with Rip and Henry just before the gates to Everdon Park, but on that narrow road there was no question of passing. Once through the gate, however, the wide, smooth, gently curving avenue made it a pure test of speed.

Rip, it was clear, had pressed his team too hard. When he asked more of them, it was not there. Everdon, on the other hand, had merely to urge his team on to sweep by and up to the doors of his home.

Deirdre let out another whoop, and this time the team were too tired to object.

Grooms ran forward, and Everdon leapt down. He turned to assist Deirdre. He put his hands at her waist and swung her a full turn before setting her, breathless, on her feet.

As the grooms led both teams off to cool down, Rip and Henry came over, shaking their heads, but grinning. "It was a fine race," said Rip.

"Indeed. And most enjoyable," said Everdon.

"And damned fine driving," said Henry. "You made up the whole ten minutes, Everdon, and with a female squealing alongside."

"I most certainly did not squeal," Deirdre protested.

"Yes, you did," said Everdon. "Once just now when we won, and once when you brought the team up to speed."

Rip and Henry both gaped.

Henry said, "You let *Deirdre* drive? In a *race?*"

"She drives very well."

Both young men stared at their sister as if she'd grown pink horns.

Rip cleared his throat. "Er, sure you're right, Everdon. Nothing against Deirdre and all that, but I'd rather this didn't get out, don't you know. Beaten by you is one thing. Beaten by a chit of a girl . . ."

Deirdre's heart was touched by his anguish. She put her hand on his arm. "I only drove for a little way, to warm up the horses, Rip. It was Everdon's fine handling that did the job."

Rip laughed in relief. "Bound to be. Know what? You're a good little thing, Dee. Take my advice. Marry this one."

Deirdre couldn't even take offense to that. Rip would urge her to marry any man who could acquit himself well in sporting activities, regardless of any other qualities.

The coach would be some time behind them, and so they all made their way into the house.

Everdon Park House was, as Everdon had once said, quite small. It was a plain three-story cube without wings. As a consequence it had solidity, and Deirdre rather liked that. Moreover, the architect had been skilled, and the lines of the building were very elegant. Without facade or addition, they were unspoiled.

As they mounted the five steps to the front door, she turned to Everdon. "I like your house."

"Thank you. I'm quite fond of it myself, though it will have to be enlarged. Even a moderate house party such as I have assembled now stretches its capabilities. I hope to do it without destroying its purity."

They entered a pleasant square hall with tiled floor and paneled walls. In a somewhat strange voice, Everdon said, "I fear its capacity is going to be stretched a little further."

Deirdre looked around to see a young gentleman emerge from a room. He was tall, thin, and dressed amazingly in yellow. Dull yellow jacket, bright yellow pantaloons, yellow and bronze cravat ... As his hair was chick yellow curls, the impression was a little overwhelming.

"Deirdre," said Everdon, "may I introduce my cousin, Kevin Renfrew, also known as the Daffodil Dandy. Kevin, this is Lady Deirdre Stowe, and her brothers, Lord Ripon and Mr. Henry Stowe."

The young men all greeted one another with familiarity, so Deirdre had to assume this apparition led a moderately normal social life.

He bowed to her. "Lady Deirdre. Charmed. Came to lend a hand." His face was too long and thin to be good-looking, but there was an amiable charm in his expression. Deirdre suspected he might be simple.

They shook hands. Servants came forward to take away outer garments.

Everdon said to his cousin, "Lend a hand? With what, pray?" But he didn't sound annoyed, merely resigned.

"Oh, anything," said Renfrew vaguely. "Did you know you have mayapples growing in the sunken garden?"

Everdon steered them all into a room, which turned out to be a wainscoted saloon hung with family portraits and furnished in a motley manner. The contents seemed to be the casual accumulation of generations, and as such, it held an air of being well used and comfortable, rather than a room reserved for guests. Deirdre rather liked it.

"No," Everdon said to Renfrew. "I did not know about mayapples, but then I don't know the half of what I have in the garden."

"Quite rare, mayapple is. Your gardener was going to pull them up."

"I assume he's changed his mind."

"Oh yes. Very reasonable sort of fellow."

"I've always found him rather jealous of his territory."

Deirdre had been admiring a stunning portrait of the dowager as a young bride with wicked, flashing eyes. Now she turned, fascinated by the strange conversation.

"And how's Ian?" Everdon was asking. "The last I heard, he'd rallied a little."

"Yes. Stopped by there the other day, but didn't stay. Fusses him to know I'm next in line."

This was said without resentment, but Deirdre could sympathize with Sir Ian Renfrew, the Daffodil Dandy's older brother. She'd heard talk of the sad case; Sir Ian was stricken by a wasting disease from which he would not, it seemed, recover. Not yet thirty, he would leave a widow and three young girls. No wonder the thought of the Daffodil Dandy inheriting his property and the responsibility for his family was bad for his health.

"Stopped by?" asked Everdon. "Have you not been there these last months?"

"No. Like I say, it does him more harm than good." Renfrew's lips quirked in a sad little smile. "Though I did wonder whether my hanging around might perk him up, give him even more need to get well. There's nothing in it, though. He's done for, Don. Don't seem any point in fussing him. I've been in the Shires most of the year, doing over a place Verderan inherited there."

"Piers Verderan? The Dark Angel? You've been decorating a house for him?" Even Everdon was beginning to sound bemused.

"Yes." Kevin Renfrew drifted over to a pier table and absently rearranged the three figurines that stood on it. "Rather interesting actually," he said. "The foundation in the northwest corner is crumbling."

"Then if you were doing the house over, you should have looked to it."

"Not there. Here," said Renfrew. "I'm reading about gilding." With that he wandered off.

Deirdre shared a hilarious look with her brothers. Everdon, however, rang the bell.

When his butler appeared, he gave orders for refreshments, but then said, "Has the foundation been checked?"

"I did take the liberty of making that arrangement, milord. It appears work is necessary."

"Put it in hand, then." Everdon turned to Deirdre. "I think you would like to remove the dust before tea. I'll have a maid take you to your room."

Deirdre had been staring at the three figurines that Kevin Renfrew had rearranged, realizing with astonishment that their new placement was subtly, but clearly, more pleasing than the old. Now she started, and glanced in the mirror above the pier table. She gasped at the sight she presented. She was turned almost dun brown with dust, and her hair was escaping its pins and the bonnet in all directions. "Heavens! I look a perfect sight!"

Everdon's eyes met hers in the mirror. "Yes, you do." His smile, however, gave the words quite a different meaning, and their gaze held for a breathless moment.

Deirdre fled the room in a flustered state, flustered by more than casual flattery. The assaults on her stability seemed never-ending. She'd end up as daft as that Daffodil Dandy.

What was she to make of Kevin Renfrew? He appeared to be lacking a large portion of his wits, and yet Everdon had taken his words about the foundation perfectly seriously. And with reason.

She wondered if there *were* mayapples in the sunken garden.

As she took off her bonnet and cloak in her small but pleasant room, she felt a new range of insecurities.

She hadn't anticipated the effect of being in Everdon's home. It drew her to him in a disturbing way. She certainly hadn't anticipated the introduction of a fey daffodil. There was something in the air in this house.

It felt like a place where things could change.

9

By the next day, however, Deirdre had decided that her anxieties had been the result of weariness, or too much sun. Everdon's home was surprisingly simple and old-fashioned, but it was comfortable and well run. There were no strange undertones at all.

Everdon had a number of matters awaiting his attention as he had not spent more than a night here for some months, and so he arranged for his guests' comfort, then disappeared. Deirdre had expected an attempt to keep her away from Howard, and was perplexed that this was not so.

Howard, too, perplexed her. Perhaps it was that he was away from his cottage, but he was not himself; for one thing, he did not appear to be working at all. He was completely available for walks in the grounds, games of cards, and even angling. Deirdre knew she should have been delighted by this evidence that he could enjoy such normal pursuits, but it just made her feel even more uneasy.

Perhaps that was because she had the impression that Howard was not really enjoying himself, but joining in these activities for a purpose.

He even agreed to join Rip and Henry in cricket practice.

As she stood in the shade by the lawn, watching Howard face a cricket ball tossed by Rip, the Daffodil Dandy appeared at her side. "Clever chap, that."

156

"Yes. Brilliant." Her heart did not, however, swell with pride. Anyone coherent would appear brilliant to Kevin Renfrew.

"Cares a lot about you."

"Do you think so?" she said, heart swelling despite her earlier thoughts.

"Oh yes. Wouldn't be out here knocking a ball about if he didn't. Very purposeful man." He wandered off to stand by Henry, though whether he was fielding or not was unclear.

Deirdre looked at Howard and realized that, of course, he had no interest in knocking balls about. And his purpose was plain—he was trying to please her, poor lamb.

When the game was over, she linked arms with him as they wandered over to the table where a footman was serving ale and lemonade. "I'm sure you must be longing to return to your studies, Howard."

"True, but I don't mind taking a few days off. I have things to think about."

"If that's what you want, of course. But I just wanted you to know that I don't expect you to dance attendance on me. I know how important your work is."

He smiled warmly and patted her hand. "I know you do. That's one reason I know we'll suit. I probably will spend some time in my room this afternoon making some notes. That Renfrew chap said some interesting things this morning about negative numbers."

"Kevin Renfrew?" Deirdre asked blankly.

"Yes. Strange fellow. Didn't know what he was saying, of course, but triggered an idea or two."

So, after luncheon, Deirdre was deserted. She took the opportunity to visit Lucetta. Here, even more than in Missinger, it was Lucetta's duty to be with Lady Harby, but on this occasion Deirdre's mother had developed a headache and was lying down in her room.

Deirdre went into the dowager's suite and looked around with pleasure. "Oh, how lovely!"

Lucetta smiled. "I think so. My husband had it decorated this way for me, to remind me of home."

The boudoir was painted white, and the floor was tiled in a mosaic of reds and golds. Gilt-framed pictures of Spanish scenes decorated the walls, and ornate grilles covered the two long windows, softening and diffusing the bright sun.

"In Cordoba, where I grew up, there is a lot of Moorish influence," said Lucetta. "There is also a lot of sun, so we hide from it. In the English winter those screens come down so I can appreciate what sunlight the good Lord sends this northern land."

Deirdre looked at a bas-relief of the Madonna and child. "Was it hard to leave your land, your family?"

"It was not easy," admitted Lucetta, "and my English was not good then. When I had Marco, I spoke to him almost entirely in Spanish, which is how he came to know the language so well. By the time Richard was born, it was less the case. And then he was the one to go to Spain . . ."

Lucetta's eyes turned to a small portrait on the wall, and Deirdre looked, too. It showed a smiling man in regimentals, clearly Everdon's brother, who had died at Vittoria. He and Everdon must have been very different, for Richard Renfrew looked more like Kevin—a longer face and paler coloring.

"I'm glad the war is over," said Deirdre, feeling it was an inadequate expression of sympathy, but not knowing what else to say.

"As are we all. My poor Spain . . . But," Lucetta said more briskly, "it was doubtless a blessing that I came north with Marco's father and escaped the horrors."

Deirdre wandered the room thoughtfully. "I'm not

sure if I could leave England to live in a foreign land."

"Not even with Howard?"

Deirdre paused and frowned. "But why would he want to leave?"

"Who can say? There are famous universities in Germany, for example. He might wish to study there."

Deirdre felt a creeping unease. "Then I suppose I would go."

"Of course you would. Marriage is always a cause of change, and a change of country could be part of it. I found it hard to come to England, but I would have found it harder to have separated from John."

She indicated another, larger portrait, and Deirdre went over to look at Everdon's father.

"He was so special to me," Lucetta said softly. "Only a poet could have expressed it. You can see that he was not terribly handsome, nor did he have a golden tongue. He had honest eyes, though, and what they said to me was very precious."

Deirdre felt tears in her eyes as she looked at the portrait. John Renfrew, Earl of Everdon, had been a young man when this was done, but his wigless state showed a hairline that already receded. His face was long, rather like his second son's and Kevin Renfrew's, and his mouth was wide and humorous. His blue eyes were doubtless honest, but they were saying little of importance to the portrait painter. But he had been deeply loved, and Deirdre did not doubt he had loved deeply in return. Lucetta would have left her home for nothing less.

"Everdon doesn't look like him," she said.

"No, but there is a great deal of John in Marco. Marco looks just like my family, but he has the English restraint. It can be dangerous. He holds things in, covers them up, so that even those who love him

do not see what is inside. My family," she added
dryly, "concealed nothing, held back nothing."

Deirdre moved on to a portrait of a young Don
Juan, done perhaps when he was twenty or so. He
was standing by a tree in country clothes, riding crop
in hand. His hair was rather long and curling, and
his dark eyes bright with laughter. His stance was
both relaxed and supremely confident. He was handsome now, but something had disappeared that had
been caught in this picture. A sense of invulnerabil-
ity, perhaps.

"That was done in 1804, when he was little older
than you, Deirdre. Just before his father died."

Was that what had tarnished some of the gold?
Grief and responsibility?

Lucetta spoke again, deliberately. "And before his
marriage, of course."

Deirdre looked around. "Is there a portrait of his
first wife here?" Then she could have bitten her
tongue for such a tactless, stupid question.

"I would hardly keep one," said Lucetta dryly.
"There was a miniature. I do not know where it
went. Perhaps it was returned to her family with the
rest of her possessions."

Deirdre knew this subject was best left alone, but
she felt a pressing need to know more. Lucetta, she
was sure, had raised the subject with some purpose.
She faced the dowager. "He must have been very
young when they married."

Lucetta looked down at the embroidery in her
hands. "He was twenty. She was seventeen."

"So young?" Deirdre said in surprise. "Why . . . ?"
She swallowed what she had been about to say.

"Why did I permit it?" Lucetta queried wryly.
"You are contemplating marriage at eighteen, Deir-
dre." She sighed. "But you are right, it was not wise.
But they were very much in love."

Deirdre felt a stab of pain at that. "I understand she was very beautiful."

"Very."

Deirdre hesitated to ask, but she had to know. "What happened?"

Lucetta laid down her work and looked up. "You will have to ask Marco. I do not know the whole, and it is not my story to tell. But Iphegenia Brandon was a wild flame destined to burn bright and fast. I should have realized that. Soon after the marriage, she made it clear that she found Marco lacking in some essential way."

"I find that hard to believe." The words escaped Deirdre before discretion could stop them. She colored and turned away from Lucetta's perceptive eyes. "He's handsome and charming," she added quickly. "What else did she want?"

"What else do you want?"

The words were a challenge.

Deirdre sucked in a deep breath, but something in the moment demanded honesty. "I want to be crucial to someone's life," she said quietly.

"Ah."

Lucetta said nothing more, and so Deirdre turned. Her friend was now sewing calmly. "Ah? is that all you're going to say?"

Lucetta glanced up. "What else is there to say? I do not know if you are crucial to the life of Marco or Howard Dunstable."

"Everdon would scarcely notice if I were to disappear," Deirdre said firmly. "Howard certainly would. Then he'd never get his eggs cooked correctly." She bit her lip. More words she wished unsaid. "I mean, that's not important. It's just that he needs me in so many little ways. He'd be miserable without me, and then he'd never get his work done, and I'm sure it's dreadfully important . . ."

"I'm sure it is, too," said Lucetta calmly. "You

didn't bring any needlework with you? If you wish to sew here with me, you will always be welcome."

"Thank you," said Deirdre, feeling that she had yet again failed to convey the reality of her relationship with Howard. Why was it always so difficult? "I think I need a walk just now, though."

"Very well." As Deirdre turned to go, Lucetta picked up a piece of paper. "This account needs to go to Marco. Do you think you could put it in his study?"

Deirdre took it. "Yes, of course." She was no fool. She knew Lucetta was hoping Everdon would be there, and was throwing them together. But Deirdre did not intend to avoid him. To avoid him would be to admit that being with him could endanger her feelings for Howard. That was simply not true.

All the same, when she knocked on his study door and his voice said, "Enter," she felt a frisson of doubt.

He was sitting behind a desk thick with ledgers and papers. He was not alone. A plump young man rose, blushing, from behind another desk.

Everdon rose, too, a smile lighting his face. "Deirdre. What a delightful excuse to rest from my labors. Morrow, why don't you walk down to the agent's cottage and see if he has those missing records? The fresh air will do you good."

The young man's eyes flickered between them, and he made himself scarce. He carefully left the door wide open.

"A young gentleman of unimpeachable rectitude," remarked Everdon with a smile. "I don't know how he bears with me."

Deirdre held out the paper. "Your mother asked me to give you this."

He took it and raised a brow. "She clearly thinks I've been neglecting you."

"Not at all . . ."

"Don't you think so?"

"No."

He tapped the paper thoughtfully. "Where's Dunstable?"

"Working. He had an insight."

"Excellent."

Deirdre considered the earl suspiciously. She didn't forget the way he'd encouraged Howard on his little jaunt out of Reading.

He smiled blandly. "I want all my guests to be happy here. Do you have everything you need?"

"Yes, thank you."

He tossed down the account unread. "Have you had the grand tour of the house? No? Come on."

Deirdre found herself swept along, but wasn't reluctant. She was feeling edgy and unable to settle. A tour of the house seemed just the ticket, and in such a small and crowded building, there could be no real danger.

She had, of course, seen the drawing room, the dining room, and the breakfast room, but he took her through them again, pointing out items of interest. For the first time she realized how unplanned the rooms were, how old most of the decor and furnishings.

"No one in your family seems to have been inclined to modernization," she remarked.

"No. The last major work done inside the house was my mother's rooms. Would you want to change everything?"

The question seemed to have singular importance, but Deirdre responded lightly. "No. I think it charming."

"That's as well. It would cost the earth."

She gave him an uneasy look, but he said nothing more.

They looked in the library, which was only moderately stocked, and gave nodding recognition to a small, bleak reception room that was surely only used for unwanted visitors.

Then they went to the back of the house to a small garden room. This had glass doors that opened onto a tiled patio edged on two sides by rose trellises. Beyond was the west lawn.

"This is lovely," Deirdre said, and leaned over to smell a red rose. It was strongly perfumed, almost too strongly.

He plucked a pink one and gave it to her. "Red roses are for my mother. This will suit you better."

She held it close to her nose and found the perfume was indeed more subtle and to her taste. She glanced at him over the petals. "You think you know me very well, don't you?"

He shook his head. "No, Deirdre. I don't know you at all. Otherwise I would be able to make you do just as I wish."

She shivered. "I'd hate that."

He smiled. "I don't think I'd care for it much either. Keep your secrets, *querida*. It doesn't take magical powers to see that red is not your color."

He led the way back into the darker coolness of the house. As Deirdre passed a chaise in the garden room, she noticed that it was quite badly frayed along one edge so that the stuffing would soon start to escape. Distracted by that, she almost tripped when the toe of her slipper snagged a hole in the carpet.

Everdon did not see her stumble, but Deirdre was made strongly aware that his house was, in fact, quite shabby. After a hesitation, she asked, "Why did you mention cost before? You are surely rich enough to refurbish your house if you should wish."

They had moved into the hall and begun to mount the stairs. "If I wished, of course. But it is a matter of priorities. Foundations and land drainage come first.

That ugly picture, by the way, is a portrait of me as a baby by Aunt Jane."

Though she had not received a satisfactory answer, Deirdre politely paused to study the strange little oil. "How fortunate that your eyes eventually settled in their correct positions."

"Yes, wasn't it? And that slightly better painting is her depiction of the park before my father landscaped it."

In this picture, Everdon Park House stood square in the middle of a small formal garden and flat meadows, peopled by rather unlikely cows. It looked stark.

"I think the changes were an improvement," she said.

"It's hard to tell. Don't forget, Aunt Jane painted that picture, too. The better artwork is along here."

A corridor with windows along one side formed a small gallery. Deirdre inspected the obligatory ancestors, noting the general trend toward the long, thin Renfrew face. Then she came across a family portrait surely executed not long before Everdon's father's death.

The former earl stood proudly behind the chair in which Lucetta sat, a Lucetta unfamiliar to Deirdre. She was some ten years younger, of course, but she fairly sizzled with life. Her gown was white muslin, but she wore a vivid red and black shawl as a sash, and a red rose in her black hair. Her husband had his hand on her shoulder, and her hand covered his.

She was looking up at her sons, who stood close together, smiling at their parents. It was a startlingly cohesive group, and it brought tears to Deirdre's eyes to think it had been torn apart.

As if he knew, Everdon said, "Within the year he was dead."

"How?" she whispered.

"Typhus, probably caught from a prisoner when he

was serving as magistrate. He cared too much. Sometimes, if he wasn't satisfied with what happened in court, he would go to the jail to question a felon further. He died in three days."

Impulsively Deirdre turned and took his hand. He returned her grip, and they stood there, looking at each other.

He drew her along the corridor, swung open a door, and then released her hand. He stood back to let her precede him.

Deirdre walked through, then halted.

"My bedroom," he said, confirming her fears. He leaned, arms crossed, in the open doorway, not blocking her escape.

Daring her.

That powerful moment of shared grief had left Deirdre shaken and adrift. She walked a few paces farther into the lion's den but promised herself that if he closed the door, she'd scream.

"A pleasing chamber," she said, tolerably calmly, "but yet again in the old style."

"As you say," he replied, in a tone that did not sound particularly natural. "Lucetta's suite is, of course, next door. My first wife and I felt no need of separate rooms, but perhaps that is not wise. This time we will knock through a door on the other side. There would be no question, of course, of Lucetta moving out of those rooms, or leaving the house."

"No, of course not," said Deirdre. Then she looked at him sharply. " 'We'?" Her heart was running at an alarming rate, which was doubtless why she felt rather light-headed.

"There will presumably be a 'we' when the matter arises. Do you want to see the kitchens or the attics? Otherwise, I'm afraid the tour is over."

Silence fell except for the birdsong floating in through the open window.

Deirdre broke the moment by turning away to look

down the wide drive along which they'd raced just a few days before. She was finding it remarkably difficult to think clearly, and yet knew she must. She turned and saw a small bookshelf by his bed. Chaucer, something Spanish, Locke and Southey's *Life of Nelson.* She noted that his bed hangings were threadbare in places.

She faced him. "I've decided what question I want an honest answer to."

For once, she noted with satisfaction, she'd thrown him off balance. "Question?" he queried in wary perplexity.

"The billiard game," she reminded him. "You owe me an answer."

"Ah, yes." He moved away from the doorway, and came to stand a few feet away. "And your question, *mia?*"

Deirdre summoned her courage, for the question was undoubtedly impertinent. "Why is money a matter of concern to you? Are you not as rich as it would seem?"

"That's two questions," he pointed out, but then shrugged. "I am, in a sense, not as rich as it would seem. Land is wealth, and I still have plenty of land, but much of the income has to go back into it. But that doesn't answer your question, does it? You asked why. The answer is, quite simply, the park."

He gestured toward the view of the beautiful park. "When my father took it into his head to re-create this corner of Northamptonshire, he spared no expense. It became a madness with him. It is very beautiful, but it almost ruined us all. When he died I found immense debts and mortgages. We have reclaimed everything, but there is still not an abundance of ready money. New furnishings have not been particularly high on my list of priorities."

"I'm not surprised. It must have been hard to cope with all that when you were so young."

"Yes, but it was losing my father that was harder."

She felt the strongest urge to go to him and hold him, as if that would comfort him. It was silly, for he was a grown man, and Don Juan, but if it hadn't been for Howard, she might well have done it.

Instead she moved toward the door. "I must go, my lord. Thank you for the tour."

"Thank you for your company, Deirdre."

Deirdre found herself inexplicably frozen, facing him across the faded carpet. "I'm sorry for asking such a question."

"Don't be. I give you carte blanche. You may ask me anything."

"Do you not have anything of which you are ashamed?" she asked in a spurt of irritation.

"Yes."

"What?"

He laughed. "A low blow, indeed. Your carte blanche has just been rescinded. You can't go on fishing expeditions. Do you have a precise question?"

Deirdre didn't, unless it was to ask why she was still in this dangerous room, alone with him.

After a moment, he came carefully toward her. "If you were to hit me, *cara*," he said softly, "I'd be obliged to kiss you."

Oh, so that was why. Deirdre took a deep breath, made a fist, and thumped him in the chest.

His hands settled on her shoulders, gently sensitive to her skin and nerves. "You are a very violent young woman." He laid his lips softly over hers.

Deirdre stood there, heart racing, wondering what on earth she was doing. This was wrong. This wasn't what she wanted. Not really. Her lips moved against his.

His hands slid up her neck and cradled the back of her head, turning it slightly to make a more interesting angle, to deepen the intimacy.

Her hands were held defensively against his chest,

poised virtuously to push him away. They lacked all power. Then strength returned, but only to slide up to his shoulders, and from there to the soft edges of his hair and the skin of his neck beneath ...

He opened his lips. Instinctively she did the same, as if speaking against him softly of secrets. Their breath mingled, moist and warm, an intimate taste she had never experienced before. Openmouthed, he just brushed his lips against hers, sharing, somehow, more than breath.

She sobbed softly somewhere in the back of her throat.

He drew back, heavy-lidded, and trailed a thumb along her jaw. "You taste of eternity, Deirdre Stowe."

Deirdre swallowed, trembling. "It's just expertise. Yours, I mean, not mine."

"No."

He made no move, but Deirdre knew that in time he would kiss her again, more deeply, more shatteringly, and she wanted it.

At last she found the strength to push him away. "I must go."

He did not resist. "You should," he agreed.

It was like moving against a storm, but Deirdre turned and walked away.

She walked steadily out of the room and down the corridor past the paintings. She steadily made it to the safety of her own bedchamber. Once there, she collapsed, shattered, on her bed.

There was no room in her heart anymore for deception.

Howard would never kiss her like that; she would never experience with him what she had experienced with Everdon. But she was pledged to Howard, he needed her, and this hunger within her was just base lust.

She wept.

When the tears were over, she paced her room,

wishing she could leave Everdon Park today. She struggled for ways to force Everdon to end their engagement quickly, but it would have to be achieved without her having to speak to him alone. She was determined never to be alone with him again. She could not think of any way to speed matters, though, except to do as he had once suggested and compromise herself with Howard. The notion was now even more repugnant.

She simply had to trust Everdon to honor their agreement and release her.

Alarmed by the danger, however, Deirdre discarded all notion of encouraging Howard to work, and demanded his almost constant presence. She tried in every way she could to convey to the world—and in particular to Don Juan—that she and Howard were destined for perfect happiness.

"Really, Deirdre," said Howard three days later, "I don't know what's come over you. You're always hovering over me. It's almost as if you don't trust me out of your sight."

"Of course I do," Deirdre said with honesty. She never doubted Howard. She took his hand. "It's just that I like being with you." Greatly daring, she added, "Don't you like being with me?"

As Everdon had predicted, he said quickly, "Of course I do." But he pulled his hand free. "I don't think we need live in one another's pockets, though, Deirdre. You distract me."

They were in the garden, in the shade of a chestnut tree. Howard had some papers, and Deirdre had her needlework.

"I'm just sitting here, Howard. I'm not doing anything to distract you."

"You distract me just by being there." Deirdre found this rather touching until he added, "I always feel you want me to talk or something." He turned back to the papers.

Deirdre rose from the wicker chair. "Very well. I will leave you in peace."

Instead of arguing, he said, "That's a good girl."

Deirdre marched miserably toward the house. As she drew closer, however, she thought she saw someone in the window of Everdon's study. Was he watching for her, lying in wait? She hurriedly turned and walked off down the drive, tussling with her problems.

Was she wrong to want Howard to lie in wait, to seek her out? He had, after all, given her the most powerful sign of devotion by asking her to marry him.

But then, so had Everdon.

Was she wrong to be hurt that Howard wanted to concentrate on his work while Everdon seemed willing to put his responsibilities aside at any moment? She should value Howard's dedication, and despise Everdon's distractibility.

At the gatehouse, Deirdre waved to the gatekeeper, and walked out onto the narrow lane. It felt strangely liberating to leave Everdon Park, and so she strolled along the lane. There was little view here, for the hedges grew high on either side, but it was peaceful. She let her mind go blank.

Soon she came to a place where three lanes intersected, and a neat white signpost directed people to Kettering, Cranston, and Everdon Park. There seemed something strangely symbolic about this parting of the ways, so she stood beneath the post, considering her future.

She had three choices: She could marry Howard, she could marry Everdon, or she could remain a spinster. Not long ago, the prospect of being a spinster all her life would not have bothered her. She certainly did not believe that there was a special place in hell reserved for such women, where they would lead apes forevermore.

Now, however, something had been woken in her that spinsterhood would leave unsatisfied. Was it the companionship of a man, the sharing of work, the caring for his needs? Or was it the touch of a man, the moist heat of his lips, the magic he could work on her senses?

The shiver that passed through her suggested the answer.

Was this wickedness or a natural part of life?

Would Howard ever be able to satisfy that part of her that Everdon had brought to life? Surely, in time . . .

She was jerked out of her tangled thoughts by the sound of wheels. For a moment she could not decide from which direction they approached, and so she hesitated. Then a gig appeared on the Cranston Road, driven by an elderly, harsh-faced woman with a groom beside her.

The gig halted. "Are you all right, young lady?" the woman asked.

Deirdre blushed, well aware how peculiar she must look wandering about without her bonnet. "Yes, thank you, ma'am. I am a guest at Everdon Park, and I strolled down here."

The woman's face pinched. "You're the next victim, are you?" she sneered. "A fine substitute for Genie, you will be."

Deirdre just stared, and the groom sat there, arms folded, like a statue.

The woman suddenly thrust the reins into the man's hands and climbed down. She was thin, haggard, but with very good bones. "You're only a child," she said to Deirdre. "What on earth are your parents thinking of?"

"I beg your pardon?"

The woman clucked. "I am Elizabeth Brandon, my dear. Mother of Lord Everdon's betrayed first wife. I refuse to acknowledge any closer relationship than that."

Deirdre knew then that she had fallen into a dreadfully embarrassing situation. "I'm very sorry about your loss," she said faintly.

"Loss? We lost our treasure over ten years ago when that profligate enticed her from her home!"

"But he was only twenty," Deirdre protested. "And they married."

"Only twenty? But foreign," she spat. "We all know how they are abroad. Look at what happened to Genie."

Deirdre cast another desperate look at the groom, but he was doing an admirable representation of a painted dummy. Did Lady Brandon behave this way frequently? "Lady Brandon," she said gently. "I know you must be deeply distressed about your daughter, but I am sure it is unfair to place the entire blame on Lord Everdon. Your daughter did leave him of her own free will."

"What would you know of it, miss? Genie was driven away by his cruelty! He was mad for her, but once he had her, he cared nothing for her feelings, nothing at all. And she . . ." The woman's voice broke. "She . . . she loved him so. It was her love that drove her away! And what did he do or say to stop her, to get her back? Nothing. *Nothing!*"

Deirdre wanted to ask what he could have been expected to do, but knew it was wiser to keep silence. Her face must have revealed something, however, for the woman carried on. "I see he has cozened you with his fair appearance. But if he was innocent, why did he never seek a divorce?" She stabbed the air with a sharp gloved finger. "Because she would have returned to defend herself, that is why. All would have been revealed!"

Deirdre stood there, appalled, staring at that finger.

"He sent all her possessions back to us," snarled Lady Brandon. "Just swept her out of his life."

What was he supposed to do? Deirdre wondered, trying to imagine Everdon at twenty, facing that situation.

The woman suddenly sagged from anger to grief. "Then, just weeks ago, he rode up cool as you please to show us that ... that *horrible* letter ..."

Again, Deirdre wondered, what was he supposed to do? She also had some glimmering of how hard it must have been for Everdon to go to his wife's parents to break the news. She had seen no sign of his distress. As Lucetta said, he was too good at concealing things.

"Dead," the woman moaned, putting a hand to her head. "Dead so young, alone in a foreign land. And now he is finally free to destroy another young innocent."

Deirdre could see only one way to escape this horrid confrontation. "I'm afraid you have made an error, Lady Brandon. I am not to marry Everdon. I am promised to another young gentleman at Everdon Park, Howard Dunstable."

Lady Brandon frowned at her. "But I had heard ..."

"False rumors."

Lady Brandon looked her over. "More than likely. You haven't the looks for Don Juan. Genie was the most beautiful girl in England. He will marry again, though. He needs to now his family is failing all around him. Serves him right," she added viciously. "It's a judgment of God. His brother. Now his cousin. May all the Renfrews rot, every last one ..."

Deirdre backed away. "I must bid you good day—"

"You watch out for him," the woman shrieked after her. "They don't call him Don Juan without reason. He destroys women for his pleasure!"

Deirdre turned and fled back toward Everdon Park.

Once out of sight of the crossroads, she slowed to catch her breath and steady her nerves. She knew she should have sympathy for a mother's grief, but she could only think how horrible it must be for Everdon to have that kind of hate living close by all these years, how horrible it must have been to have to face them.

What on earth had happened between him and his wife all those years ago? One thing she knew, though, he did not destroy women for his pleasure.

Deirdre hurried back inside the park, hoping she was hiding her distress from the gatekeeper. Howard was still under the tree, lost in numbers. She passed him by gingerly, not wanting to speak to him just now. She smiled grimly at the very idea that he might demand her presence.

There was no watcher to be seen at the study window, and so she slipped into the house and went up to her room.

She washed her face and composed herself, looking around and wishing the walls could speak.

Why had Genie fled?

Why had Everdon never sought a divorce?

Did it, in fact, argue a guilty conscience?

10

Deirdre escaped her thoughts by seeking out her mother. Lady Harby was wise, and might be able to throw light on the situation. Lady Harby, however, was deep in the novel *Marmion*, and clearly not in the mood for company.

"Why don't you go and find Everdon, Deirdre? You've hardly spent a moment with him for days. I thought you were coming to your senses."

Deirdre scurried off to Lucetta's rooms. She, at least, was available, but Kevin Renfrew was there.

"I'm sorry," Deirdre said, prepared to retreat.

"Don't go, dear," said Lucetta. "I've seen so little of you these last days. Where's Howard?"

Deirdre took a seat cautiously. There was a strange atmosphere in the room, and the Daffodil Dandy was drooping a little. She had the uncomfortable feeling that she was intruding.

"Howard's in the garden. He's working on something, and he says I distract him just by being there." She tried to make her distractive force sound positive.

Renfrew straightened and gave her one of his vague looks. "Mathematics do tend to take over a man's head," he said. "Newton was a strange fellow. Not easy to rub along with at all."

Deirdre was beginning to realize that Kevin Renfrew's oblique comments generally carried a point, and thought she saw the direction of this one. "He *was* married, though," she said.

Renfrew nodded. "Noble woman."

Deirdre couldn't think how to respond.

Lucetta intervened. "I'm sure Howard feels guilty for neglecting you, my dear, but it is to my benefit, for now I have the pleasure of your company. I have been feeling that both Marco and I are neglecting our guests. I don't know what Marco can be thinking of."

"We're all perfectly happy," Deirdre assured her. "Rip and Henry have been enjoying cricket or the river, and today they're off to that prizefight. They will doubtless return in transports of delight, loaded with gruesome accounts of the event. Mother is plundering the novels in your library, and Howard and I have time to be together. It is all quite wonderful." Even as she said it, Deirdre could hear the strident overemphasis in her voice.

Lucetta smiled approvingly, but the smile did not quite reach her worried eyes.

Renfrew rose abruptly. "I must take my leave."

Lucetta turned to him. "God go with you, Kevin." She opened her arms, and to Deirdre's surprise, the young man accepted a hug. She knew then that his brother must be near his end. She tried to imagine what it would feel like to lose one of her sisters or brothers, especially when the death would bring so many changes and responsibilities.

Renfrew headed for the door, but stopped and faced Deirdre. There was nothing vague in his manner at all when he said, "Marry Everdon." With that he was gone.

Deirdre pulled her gaze from the closed door and looked at Lucetta. "His brother?"

Lucetta sighed. "Yes. Poor Ian. I never expected there to be so many untimely deaths in my life. Kevin has the right of it, though. You should marry Marco."

Deirdre felt bludgeoned. "I am pledged to Howard."

Lucetta threw up her hands. "My dear, what can I say? Self-sacrifice is so hard to do well."

Deirdre erupted to her feet. "I'm *not* sacrificing myself! I *love* Howard." But now the words almost choked her, and she knew they were not true.

Lucetta knew it, too; it was clear in her frowning gaze.

Deirdre said, "I met Lady Brandon a little while ago."

"Here?" Lucetta asked in surprise and dismay.

"No. Out in the road. I was walking."

"Ah. Poor woman."

"She is very bitter. Does she have reason to be?"

Lucetta sighed. "I do not think so. But if, in that bad time, Marco had shot himself, I, too, would have been bitter. It is the nature of mothers to adhere to their children's cause."

Deirdre didn't want to ask, but needed to know. "Why did he never seek a divorce?"

"As long as Richard and Ian stood in line, he had no great need to marry again, and I know he did not relish a public airing of the matter. Beyond that, I do not know. As I have said, he keeps a great deal to himself."

Deirdre wanted to ask if Everdon had done anything to drive his wife away, but she could not ask that of Lucetta.

Lucetta broke the moment by posing a question about silks for her work. Deirdre was pleased enough to leave unpleasant subjects alone. There was too much dark intensity hovering in the house today, and too many unpleasant thoughts lurking in her head . . .

A knock on the door interrupted them. A maid presented Deirdre with a note.

She opened it, puzzled. It said simply, *You are*

needed in the study. She frowned over it. It was un-signed, and she did not recognize the handwriting, but then there were few hands in this house she would recognize. She supposed it could be from the secretary—Morrow. But why would she be needed?

Lucetta was looking at her with a question in her eyes. Deirdre stood. "My mother wishes to see me," she said, knowing it made little sense.

Once in the corridor, she stood in thought, unsure what to do. Would Everdon send such a note to trap her? It simply wasn't in his style. Perhaps there was some business matter that needed her attention . . .

Then she had a startling thought. Perhaps this was Everdon's play at last. Perhaps she was to find him in a compromising situation. With whom? she wondered faintly. A maid?

Now the moment was come, she did not want to go through with it. It was going to be horribly em-barrassing, but there was more to her reluctance than that.

She was going to marry Howard—she accepted that—but as long as this mock betrothal existed, Everdon was part of her life. Once she interrupted his immorality and threw an outraged fit, it would all end. Not just the engagement, but all contact be-tween them for all eternity.

She remembered him saying, *You taste of eter-nity* . . .

But this was their agreement, and it would free him as much as it would free her; free him to seek a true bride. Deirdre wiped her damp hands on her skirt and marched off to the study.

She paused and listened. It was as if the room were empty. Could wickedness be so silent? She raised her hand to knock, but then realized that would not do at all.

She turned the knob and marched in.

Everdon looked up sharply.

He was alone.

He was seated behind his gleaming desk, cradling something in his hands. A bedraggled letter lay open before him.

The object in his hands was a miniature portrait, perhaps four inches across. He hastily put it down and rose, but he put it down faceup, and Deirdre saw that it was of a startlingly beautiful girl.

It was surely Genie, his first wife. Alerted by her expression, he flipped the picture over.

Dieirdre's chest and throat began to ache in a way that could only be eased by tears, tears she was determined not to shed.

Dear Lord, but he looked grief-stricken.

He still loved Iphegenia Brandon, the most beautiful girl in England. Even a glimpse had told Deirdre that Lady Brandon had not lied about that.

"Did you want something?" he asked in a strangely wooden voice.

Deirdre knew she should go, she should leave him to grieve in peace, but instead she closed the door gently and walked toward the desk, seeking words that would comfort him.

He held her eyes for a moment, and she could see the effort it took, then he buried his face in his hands and wept.

Deirdre froze, appalled. More than anything in her life, she wanted to enclose him in her arms as she would a hurt child. All her civilized instincts, however, told her she must ignore something of which he would surely be ashamed.

She began to edge back toward the door.

He looked up, grimaced, and wiped his face with his handkerchief. "My apologies. My damned Spanish half escapes every now and then." He rose sharply to his feet and went to a table to pour himself a glass of brandy. He knocked it back and poured another.

He looked at her. "Want some?"

She shook her head.

"Steadies the nerves." His voice was still rough with emotion.

There was a silver snuffbox on his desk. Deirdre picked it up, and with unsteady hands, presented it to him. He took it, placed it by the brandy decanter, and opened it.

"Your wrist, if you please," he said, still in a voice unlike his usual mellow tones.

Deirdre looked, puzzled, at her wrists, then extended her right hand. He captured it, turned it, and placed some snuff on the pale, veined underside. His hand warm beneath hers, he raised her wrist to inhale first in one nostril, then the other. His eyes closed as he savored the effect. Deirdre stared at him, wondering how her wrist could be so intimately connected to her heart.

Eyes still closed, he said, "If you don't intend to marry me, Deirdre, you should not have come here today."

Deirdre glanced anxiously at the closed door. "It won't matter."

His eyes opened. "That's not what I mean."

He pulled her into his arms and kissed her.

It was nothing like any kiss Deirdre had experienced before. It was an elemental force that offered no escape.

He trapped and molded her to him in a shockingly intimate way. His hungry lips demanded union, a union her body craved. She was a willing puppet in the arms of a master of sensuality.

She pressed closer and opened her lips; he deepened his burning possession. She ceased to be a separate person and became part of him, and he part of her. She had a shattering insight of how it would feel to be skin to skin and more.

And wanted it.

Alarmed at last, she pushed away.

He resisted.

She struggled in his arms.

Abruptly he let her go.

Deirdre staggered back. She collided with a chair and collapsed into it, staring at her wild-eyed lover.

Passion. She had never known such passion existed.

He drew on control like a dark cloak. "Should I apologize?"

She hugged herself and shook her head. Apologies certainly didn't seem appropriate.

"Have I disgusted you?"

She shook her head again. Words just didn't seem possible.

"Frightened you?"

Another shake of the head. Yes, she was frightened, but not of him.

He moved swiftly to kneel in front of her and captured her hands. "Speak to me, *cara*. You're frightening *me*."

Words were still impossible, but she squeezed gently on his hands. He loosed her fingers and placed a kiss first on one palm, then the other. "I can't let you marry Dunstable."

That broke the dam. "You can't stop me." But when she tugged her hands free of his, it was with reluctance.

"I could seduce you. Here. Now."

Deirdre looked into his dark, passionate eyes and knew it was the truth. "You won't."

"No," he said softly. "I won't." He recaptured her hands, and it was as if he tried to seize her soul. "Why in God's name are you so bent on marrying him?"

"Because he *needs* me."

"I need you, too."

"Not as he does, and I have given my word.

Would *you* break your word? What good are you to me, to any woman, if you would pledge your word and then break it?"

He shook his head. "It's not that kind of situation, *mia*."

"Is it not? You have powers to attract, Don Juan, and I am attracted. I confess it. But am I to turn away from Howard to chase the first more attractive man who crosses my path? Is that honor? That, surely, is what your wife did." She used it as a weapon and saw it strike home.

"You could be right," he said steadily. "But I gave Genie cause to leave me, as Dunstable is giving you cause to leave him. I do not blame her."

"What cause?" she asked.

He shook his head. "It's ancient history. But in my way I loved Genie, Deirdre, and Howard does not love you."

"Yes, he *does*." Deirdre was no longer quite sure of this, but what else could she say? In honor she was bound to Howard.

"No, he doesn't love you," said Everdon firmly. "If I prove it to you, will you marry me?"

How could she believe that a man like Everdon really wanted to marry her? As Lady Brandon had said, his taste ran to beauty. But clearly in his belief that she should not marry Howard, he would do anything, even to pretending to love her.

Deirdre had this horrifying image of them all going in circles saying conventional, meaningless things, spiraling down into disaster. She rose to face him. "You won't be able to prove that Howard doesn't love me, because it isn't true."

"But if I do?"

"I still won't promise to marry you. Our betrothal is a sham. We always intended to end it."

He took a deep breath and ran his hands through his hair. "If I prove to you that Dunstable doesn't love you, will you at least promise not to marry him? Please, Deirdre."

She looked down at her hands. "He asked me to marry him. Why would he do that if he doesn't love me?"

"You find him housekeepers."

It was like a sword to the heart. She looked up at him, knowing the pain of it would be on her face.

He met her eyes. "Go on, hit me. I'm owed one for that kiss."

She swallowed tears. "No, I gave you that kiss. But can't you see, Don? You're trying to make me like Genie. The man she ran away with—I don't know who he was—he probably said to her the things you say to me, and played on her desires and disappointments as you play on mine. But I will *not* be like Genie. There has to be honor above desire. I have given my word to Howard, and I will keep it."

She turned and fled the room. She raced to her bedroom to collapse on the bed there, and weep with a depth and agony she had never believed possible.

The pain she felt must surely be the pain of a broken heart.

Back in his study, Everdon sank into his chair and buried his face in his hands. He was determined not to weep again. No wonder Deirdre wanted nothing to do with him after such an un-British display of emotion.

But that wasn't what had driven her away.

You're trying to make me like Genie.

Was that what he was trying to do? Genie had said she loved him, had agreed to marry him, had tangled with him in bed in some of the most frighteningly intense passion he had ever known. Then she had met someone who pleased her better and left, leaving only a note saying she was bored, and unhappy, and couldn't be expected to stay.

Was he asking Deirdre to do the same thing?

There has to be honor above desire.

But he had loved Genie almost beyond reason. He had honestly tried to cherish her. Dunstable did not love and cherish Deirdre.

He moved his hands and flipped the miniature. Genie looked up at him with that heavy-lidded, secretive gaze that had driven him mad with desire. Her soft, perfect lips were parted slightly as if ready for a kiss. And she'd been a virgin when this had been done.

Abruptly he swept the miniature away to shatter against the far wall.

But then he regained his English sangfroid, and carefully picked up the pieces and placed them in a drawer.

As he did so, he saw a piece of paper on the floor and realized Deirdre must have dropped it. He picked it up and found the note. He recognized the writing.

Kevin. What the devil had this been about?

He'd shown Kevin the letter he'd just received. What a hellish postbag today's had turned out to be—a letter about Ian's failing, and Genie's last words.

He had not received the consolation he had expected. Kevin had his mind on his own problems, true, but it wasn't that. . . .

He picked up the letter—another stained and weary missive from Greece, delayed even more than the news of Genie's death, for this had been written shortly before. It shocked him how weak and wandering her writing was, but the words shocked him more.

> . . . *How could you have cast me off, Don? It was always you. I didn't really want to leave, but you worked so hard, it was no fun. You should have come*

for me, and beat me if I strayed. Di Pozzinari whipped me if I looked at another man, and I stayed with him. Next to you, I loved him best. He died. Why did he die?

Why wouldn't you change for me? We were so happy until you became so dull. Mortgages. Debts. Crops. Rents. I hate them all. I only wanted to enjoy life . . .

Why didn't you love me? You couldn't expect me to stay when you were unkind. You were supposed to come after me . . .

It wandered on in this vein over the whole sheet, crossed, and the message kept repeating. *You were supposed to come after me.*

In his pain and tortured pride, it had never occurred to him to chase after his faithless wife. It had certainly never occurred to him to drag her home and whip her into submission. He had thought she wanted to be free.

Kevin had only said, "Poor Genie. She loved the wrong man." What the devil had that meant?

Everdon took the letter up to his mother.

Lucetta read it soberly. "She was doubtless out of her mind. The pox does that."

"But there's truth there. Why did it never occur to me to drag her back?"

"Marco, you were twenty years old. She rejected you, hurt you, made a cuckold of you. If you had made any move to rush off to the Continent after her, I would have had you forcibly restrained."

That summoned a bitter laugh. "But don't you see . . .?" He went over to the window and stared out. She thought he would say nothing more, and looked with bitter dislike at the straggly writing on the page.

"I didn't want her back." It was said so softly that

she almost missed it. His voice was clearer when he said, "My pride was hurt, and I missed the passion, but I'd tired of her tantrums. I abandoned her just as much as she abandoned me. And it killed her."

"Ten years later."

"She never would have died as she did if I'd kept her safe."

"With a whip?" Lucetta asked caustically.

He turned and leaned against the wall, but his face was shielded. "Perhaps that's what she liked. Wasn't it my duty as her husband to give her what she liked?"

"No." He frightened her in this mood. Her husband had sometimes, rarely, retreated into this kind of shell, but Lucetta had known ways of breaking through her husband's icy shield that she could not use with her son.

"I was her husband," he said quietly, "and I should have tried harder to be what she needed. That, surely, is part of the marriage bond. I knew she wanted gaiety and excitement, but I trapped her here in this decrepit house."

"You had no choice. If you'd lived as she wanted, we'd all be in the workhouse."

"So," he continued as if she hadn't spoken, "she realized she didn't like me anymore, and left, and I hated her for it. But I already knew I didn't like her anymore, and I'd abandoned her in spirit, if not in fact. As Deirdre said, doesn't honor require that we not take the easy way out once we have given our word?"

"What has Deirdre to do with this?"

"She has accused me, convincingly, of trying to do to her what di Pozzinari did to Genie in seducing her away from me."

Lucetta tossed down the letter. "Deirdre and Dunstable are not yet married."

"And does that make it right?"

"Yes."

He rubbed a hand over his haggard face. "I don't know what's right and wrong anymore."

"*Santísima!*" Lucetta spat, and for her it was swearing. It brought his head up, surprised. "Can you break their engagement?" she demanded.

"Yes."

"Then do it. If you can do it, there were deep flaws there anyway. As there were in your marriage. But don't force her into marrying you."

"It will hurt her."

"Think of it as the surgeon's knife."

"Lord, but I have no taste for it."

"Think of it as reparation then. You did not rescue Genie, but you can rescue Deirdre."

"With a whip?" he said with distaste.

"At the very least, with a scalpel."

Everdon returned to his study and spent some time in thought. Then, with a sigh, he sent a footman with a message for Howard Dunstable. He paced the room in restless indecision as he waited for the man to come.

Then Dunstable entered. "Yes, my lord?"

The man's bland unawareness of any undertones decided Everdon on his course.

"Have a seat, Dunstable. Brandy? Wine?" The amenities over, Everdon looked at the man, trying to dislike him and failing. He didn't like him, but Dunstable was merely charting his own course.

"I have been thinking on your comments about patronage of the sciences," Everdon said at last. "I would like to do what I can to facilitate your work."

Dunstable straightened. "I confess, I am surprised."

"Are you? Why?"

"I didn't think you liked me."

"Liking has little to do with it. You don't like me,

but you are willing to take my money. From speaking with you, and from inquiries I've made, I'm convinced you have a remarkable ability. It deserves to progress unhindered. I am willing to cover generous living costs that should ensure your comfort—and therefore a lack of distractions. I will also allow for traveling expenses. I understand there are interesting centers of mathematics on the Continent."

Dunstable blinked. "That is remarkably generous. Where am I to live? Here?"

"No," Everdon said firmly. "Where would you like to live?"

Dunstable considered. "Cambridge, if I don't have to teach."

"Very well."

Dunstable crossed his legs and eyed Everdon. "This will make Deirdre's life more comfortable as well."

Everdon refused to be goaded. "I suppose it may. However, I must make it clear that I will provide enough funds for a single man to live well. There will be no extra allowance for wife and children. How you stretch the money is up to you."

They studied each other calculatingly. Everdon remembered: logarithmic tables at twenty paces.

Then Dunstable said, "Children. I hadn't thought of children."

"Tends to be the natural result of marriage, and I gather you are not of a naturally celibate disposition . . ."

Dunstable's eyes narrowed. "Been spying on me?"

"Just servants' gossip, Mr. Dunstable."

"Children," mused Dunstable again.

"Noisy little creatures. Then there are doctors' bills, and schooling. Of course, I'm sure you could teach them at home . . ."

Dunstable blanched. "I don't have a gift for teaching." He showed his brilliance; it only took him a moment or two to weigh it all up. "I don't suppose Deirdre would much care for travel, actually, and some prolonged visits to the Continent would help my work."

"Certainly travel with children in tow would present problems. I have drawn up some figures and signed the agreement." Everdon pushed the paper across the desk.

Dunstable read it and nodded. "Do you want me to sign anything?"

"There is no need. You can spend the money on opium for all I care. I judge, however, that mathematics is every bit as much of an addiction as any drug."

"You could be right." Dunstable stood. "I will achieve something remarkable, my lord."

Everdon nodded. "I believe it, and you'll do better without a family."

"You're undoubtedly correct. Will you marry Deirdre, then? Is that what this is all about?"

"If she'll have me."

"Course she will. Be a fool not to. I don't see why you'd want her, though."

Everdon raised his brows. "For the same reasons as you, perhaps?"

"I hardly think you need a good housekeeper."

Everdon closed his eyes briefly. "Mr. Dunstable, the sooner we close this discussion, the better for all concerned. Please inform Deirdre of your change in plans."

"Oh, you can do that."

"No, I cannot," said Everdon with icy precision. "Let me make it clear. Our arrangement will start when you have informed Lady Deirdre of your intentions, whatever they may be, and left this house. If you intend to marry her, and she is still willing, take her with you. A coach will be at your disposal whenever you command it."

Dunstable eyed him. "I'm very tempted to call your bluff, you know."

Everdon met his gaze. "By all means."

Dunstable shrugged and left the room.

Everdon sat for a moment, fists tight on the top of his desk. Then he leapt to his feet and swept two vases, a candlestick, and an ormolu clock off the mantelpiece.

The shattering crash was remarkably satisfying.

Deirdre heard the distant crash, even in her room, and ventured out into the corridor. Her mother popped out of her room, cap askew. "What was that?"

"I don't know. A disaster in the kitchens, perhaps."

"I haven't heard kitchen noise before. Go and check, dear." Then Lady Harby focused on her daughter. "You look a bit peaked, Deirdre. Are you catching a cold?"

"Perhaps. I do feel a bit sniffly." Then to avoid her mother's shrewd eyes, Deirdre hurried down the stairs.

She met Howard coming up.

"I heard a crash," she said. "Do you know what it was?"

"No." He sounded hurried. "I want to talk to you, Deirdre. Come out into the garden."

Deirdre followed him, thinking that this was the first time she could remember Howard seeking her company. Perhaps things were finally looking up.

They went through the garden room to the rose-walled patio. Her heart began to beat faster. He'd even chosen a romantic spot. Deirdre wondered if Howard would pluck her a rose, and whether it would be pink or red.

He paced, hands behind back. "The fact is, Deirdre," he said, "I've decided it wouldn't be fair to you if we were to marry."

Deirdre stared at him. "What did you say?"

"You heard me. You're not going to be silly and accuse me of jilting you, are you?"

She sought control of her wits. "No, of course not ... But why on earth would it not be fair to me? Am I not the best judge of that?"

"Evidently not. Your parents have seen the truth all along. I can't offer you much of a life, Deirdre. There'll never be money for elegancies."

"Howard, I don't care for such things. Has Everdon been at you?"

"No," he said sharply. "You're being rather stupid about this, Deirdre. I simply don't want to marry you." Perhaps her pain showed, for he quickly added, "It's not you particularly. I don't want to marry anyone. I certainly don't want children."

Deirdre felt light-headed, but was bitterly aware that this was the most direct and meaningful conversation she and Howard had ever had. "Why did you ask me to marry you, then?"

"Are we going to hold a postmortem? Dissect the putrid corpse? Very well, if that is what you want. You are quite a tolerable woman, not much given to chatter, anxious to please, and truly grateful for even small attentions. Your family connections are excellent. I thought marriage to you would be an improvement in my circumstances. I was uncomfortable, and you seemed to add to my comfort. Now that Everdon is to be my patron, I can buy all the comfort I need."

"Everdon?" she echoed faintly.

"Yes. And if you detect ulterior motives, you are quite possibly correct. He, too, wants to marry you, doubtless for very similar reasons. He doesn't need a housekeeper, but he does need an heir. After his disastrous first marriage to a beauty, doubtless someone quiet and plain seems safer. Now, can we decently inter the corpse and get on with our lives?"

Deirdre stiffened her spine and summoned her pride. "Yes, of course." She willed her lips not to quiver and held out her hand. "I wish you all success, Howard."

He looked mildly exasperated, but he briefly shook her hand. "I'll be leaving within the hour, Deirdre. If you want my advice, take Everdon. He's a good catch for you and he won't expect too much."

Deirdre watched Howard Dunstable walk out of her life, then thumped down onto a bench, surrounded by the musky perfume of roses.

Everdon had been right, damn him. Howard had never even liked her, certainly never loved her. *Truly grateful for even small attentions.* The shame of it was brutal. She buried her burning face in her hands. She supposed that was how Everdon saw her, too.

After his disastrous first marriage to a beauty, doubtless someone quiet and plain seems safer.

That was doubtless true, and would explain the purposeful way he had pursued her. She was grateful, and safe—not the sort to run off with a foreign seducer, because no one would ever want to seduce her. Deirdre wished she, like Howard, could leave within the hour.

She rose to her feet, intending to hurry to her mother. They must return home, at the latest tomorrow. She must be allowed to end this impossible engagement.

Then she saw a figure in the garden room, and froze. She couldn't face Everdon just now. She *couldn't.* She whisked out of sight behind the trellis and ran.

She ran off into the park. Away. Away from the house. Away from Everdon, who doubtless thought he had won.

Damn him. Damn him. Damn him.

The butler closed the French doors, which someone had carelessly left open, and continued the work of seeing a guest comfortably on his way.

11

Everdon saw Dunstable off the premises. The man said he had made a clean break with Deirdre, so Everdon retreated to his study and waited anxiously for the repercussions. He wasn't sure what form they would take.

She would probably burst in on him like a termagant, blaming him for Dunstable's defection.

There was a faint hope that she would appear sweetly ready for love.

It only slowly dawned on him that she wasn't coming at all.

He made inquiries and discovered that over an hour ago, even before Dunstable had driven away, Deirdre had been seen running across the park toward the wilderness. She had appeared upset, but the undergardener who had encountered her had not thought it his place to report such a matter.

Everdon cursed and set off in pursuit. He'd known she would be a bit upset, but not deeply. Had her feelings for Dunstable run deeper than he'd thought?

He had this frightening image of her running out of the park, away down the road, out of his life. Another woman fleeing him . . . This time he would follow and bring his beloved back.

He entered the wilderness calling her name. The carefully designed area of winding paths, streams, and little craggy hills seemed populated only by birds and insects. If Deirdre was hiding here, it would be next to impossible to find her.

What if she wasn't?

He looked with concern at the small pond, which was easily deep enough for someone to drown herself in if she were determined on it, but then dismissed the notion. His Deirdre had too much courage and honor to take her life over such a matter.

But she could thoughtlessly put herself in danger.

After a last fruitless bellow of her name, Everdon hurried back to the house. He told his garden staff to keep an eye out for Lady Deirdre, particularly around the wilderness, and then had his best horse saddled. He spent the next hours riding the boundary of his estate, questioning people.

No one had seen Lady Deirdre Stowe.

He returned to the house to hear that Lady Deirdre had come in from her walk and was in her room.

Everdon almost collapsed with relief. Now the only trial was to see how she would treat him when they met.

Deirdre had huddled among some bushes when Everdon appeared, calling for her. She couldn't face him. She wished she need never face anyone again.

Both her mother and Everdon had been proved right. Howard didn't care a fig for her. What a fool she had been. No man was ever going to fall in love with ugly Deirdre Stowe. The best she could ever be was convenient.

And of course, she had made matters worse by running away; she had shown what a blow it was. If she had thought, she would have pretended she didn't care. Too late for that now.

But for Everdon to find her hiding behind a rhododendron bush with mud on her skirts and tears on her face would be the absolute bloody limit.

When he'd gone, she crept out and made her cautious way back to the house. When she passed one of the gardeners she tried to look as if she were just enjoying the sun.

Back in her room, however, she let the mask fall. She had never been so miserable in her life. It wasn't Howard's defection that was torturing her—Deirdre was aware that she was almost relieved to have that commitment ended. It was that he had ripped away the pretty illusion she had constructed about Everdon.

She tried to recall those heated moments in Everdon's study, to believe again that he had desired her, but now she could only see another clever man determined to get what he wanted. Well, she wouldn't be used anymore.

She just wanted to leave Everdon Park and put the whole sorry business behind her. She blew her nose. She would remain happily single and dedicate her life to her embroidery.

That brought a thought. What about her promise to her mother? She leapt to her feet. Her mother surely would not hold her to it now.

Would she?

Deirdre hastily washed her face and changed her gown. When she studied her reflection, her eyes were puffy, and her nose was red. She looked a fright, but then, that was nothing out of the ordinary. She *was* a fright, and always would be. She dusted a little powder on her nose to try to disguise her misery, then headed for her mother's room.

"Deirdre."

Deirdre froze as she passed the head of the stairs. She looked down to where Everdon stood, one foot raised onto the lowest step. He began to climb the stairs. She turned and ran to her mother's room, slamming the door behind her as if fiends pursued.

Lady Harby took one look, and sat her down. "What's happened, dearest?" She opened her arms.

Deirdre fell into them gratefully and burst into tears again on her mother's ample chest. Lady Harby rocked and soothed her until the tears were over. "Now, love, tell me what's amiss. It can't be worthy of all this."

Deirdre blew her nose, but she was already feeling a little better. Her mother's presence had a way of doing that. "Howard doesn't want to marry me anymore."

"Well, you can't expect me to shed tears about that, dear."

Deirdre twisted the handkerchief. "He never really wanted to. I was just ... convenient."

"Ah. Well, I never did think him a downy one. Not, at least, as far as people go. What changed his mind?"

"Don Juan," Deirdre spat. "Everdon's going to be his patron. Look after everything for him. I suppose he'll even find someone who can cook his ... his damn *eggs* right!" She started crying again, but conquered it and blew her nose fiercely. "I will *not* become a watering pot."

"Very good. Don't see what you have to cry over anyway. Now the coast's clear for you to marry Everdon."

Deirdre looked up sharply. "I will *never* marry Lord Everdon."

"Why on earth not?"

Deirdre found it hard to say. "He doesn't care for me, Mama."

"It looks to me as if he's gone to some lengths to win you."

"Convenience again. I'm just a suitable ... a suitable brood mare."

"Deirdre!" But Deirdre could see her mother was rather amused. Lady Harby considered her. "We had an agreement, Deirdre."

Deirdre flushed. "But that was different."

"What was different was that you thought you held all the cards. You had Howard in your pocket, you didn't think you could attract a suitable man, and you thought Everdon would behave badly enough to shock me. Now you find you've lost an ace. That doesn't mean you can welch on the bet."

Deirdre gasped. "Mother, this is my life. You *can't* make me marry a man I don't . . ."

"Don't like?"

Deirdre met her mother's shrewd eyes. "A man I don't want to marry."

Lady Harby nodded. "Probably not. But I'm not going to let you jilt him either. Not yet at least. Fair's fair. At last the man has a chance."

"Chance!" Deirdre wanted to indulge in a fit of the vapors. She remembered Eunice, when thwarted of something, lying on her back and drumming her heels on the floor. She finally saw the appeal. "He's still mourning his first wife, Mama! I came upon him grieving over her picture. And according to her mother, he drove her away with his cruelty. *And* he as good as admitted it! I want to leave here tomorrow, and never see Lord Everdon again."

"No," Lady Harby said flatly, and would not be moved.

Deirdre thought again of a tantrum, but remembered that when Eunice had behaved in that way, Lady Harby had thrown a jug of cold water over her. She retreated back to her room to seek some other way of sorting out her life.

Everdon stood in the middle of the wide staircase, stunned by the blank misery on Deirdre's face, by the cold way she had looked through him. God, how had his simple plan come to this moment? How had he hurt her so?

He went toward his bedroom with a good mind to

get thoroughly drunk, but instead he went to report to Lucetta.

"Your instructions have been followed, Dunstable has bowed out, and Deirdre's heart is broken. What now?"

Lucetta eyed him. "It is not entirely my fault, Marco, so I hope some of that snarling is for yourself. And for Dunstable, if it comes to that." He made a sharp movement, and she added, "If you start smashing my valuables, too, I will be very annoyed."

He beat a fist against a white wall. "I feel extremely destructive."

"It's your Spanish side, dearest. My mother kept a lot of cheap earthenware for just such occasions."

"I have never been of a violent temperament. I didn't smash anything when Genie left."

"By then, you didn't love Genie."

He turned sharply. "Are you saying I love Deirdre?"

Lucetta put down her needlework. "Mother of God, Marco. Surely you realize that!"

He collapsed into a chair. "No . . . no, I don't think . . . How can I love her? She hates me."

"I doubt that, dearest. And the two points have nothing to do with each other."

He slid back with a sigh. "Very well. You're the one with all the answers. What do I do now?"

"What did you do about Dunstable?"

"Bought him off." He explained what had happened.

Lucetta nodded. "Well done. It still would have been possible for him to have married Deirdre and lived tolerably if he'd wished to. A strange young man, and dedicated to his muse. It would never have done."

"Tell Deirdre that. She looked at me as if her heart was broken, and I was responsible. What do I do now?"

Lucetta considered him. "I don't know, but I want a promise from you, Marco."

He straightened. "That I'll make her happy? I'll do my best, though my record in that regard is not promising. Perhaps I can only cope with women on a flimsy basis."

"Don't grow maudlin on me. I want your promise that you'll tell her, and convince her, that you love her before you marry her."

He stared at her. "Why?"

"I am not a believer in the magic of words, but in this case, I think that is essential. Your word?"

He steepled his hands and rested his brow on them. "What on earth *is* love?"

"Ah, Marco, what is the sky? Love is when another person is essential. If you could wave Deirdre good-bye, even with regret, and in a few months choose another and be content, then you do not love her, and should let her go."

He looked up. "If I let her go, she'll probably never marry."

"*Dios!* You are certainly *not* to marry her out of pity. No wonder she wants nothing to do with you!"

He erupted to his feet. "I don't know what I feel, damn it!"

"Then go and find out," she snapped back. "And find something to smash at the same time!"

He stormed out and slammed the door. Huddled in her room, Deirdre heard the raised voice and the slam, and wished desperately that she were safe at home.

Everdon prowled his home restlessly, wondering what to do, what he wanted. It dawned on him that the place was unnaturally quiet, and when he saw a maid glimpse him and whip out of sight, he knew the servants, at least, were avoiding him.

He stopped and laughed bitterly. He was the kindest and most indulgent of employers. Were they now frightened of him?

He stalked to his room and rang fiercely for Joseph. In a few minutes the man came in. "Yes, milord?"

"What the devil's the matter with everyone?"

"The matter, milord?"

"The house is like a tomb."

"The young gentlemen, I understand, are at their pugilistic match. And Mr. Dunstable has left."

"What of the servants?"

Joseph looked at him with quiet confusion. "What of them, milord?"

"They are not there, damn it! I just saw one hide from me."

"They generally do, milord. It is considered proper behavior."

Everdon realized that Joseph was correct. Except when engaged in a specific duty, the servants did keep out of the way of the family and guests. He was going mad.

He ran his hands through his hair. "I suppose that is true." He glanced in a mirror and saw that he looked a state. His clothes were rumpled and his hair was standing on end. Perhaps Deirdre's painful look had not been heartbreak and reproach but mere shock at his appearance.

He stripped off his coat. He was not a man to shirk necessary steps; he had to talk to Deirdre. "Fix me up, Joseph. I need to go a-wooing."

"Yes, milord," said Joseph fervently. "It will be a pleasure.

Once more a picture of sartorial elegance, and re-sisting a disturbing tendency to wreck it all by run-ning his hands through his hair again, Everdon went first to Lady Harby's room.

He found her indulging in Walter Scott and bon-bons.

Her look, however, was direct and disapproving. "Ah, Everdon. Glad you came to see me. You have upset my daughter."

Everdon knew he was flushing like a boy. "How have I done that, pray?"

"Don't play me for a fool, my lord. I'll say no more, but I have a question."

"Yes?"

"Are you still mourning your first wife?"

"No." He looked keenly at her. "Does Deirdre think I am?"

"How should I know what Deirdre thinks?"

Everdon found he was pacing the room. "Lady Harby, I wish with all my heart to win Lady Deirdre's affections. I believe I can make her happy."

"I believe it, too, Everdon, but I tell you honestly, if you can't convince her, then the match will be off. I'll not force the girl to the altar. Nor can we stay here many days if you can't bring her around."

Beyond that, however, she would not be drawn on the matter. Everdon left with the small assurance that Lady Harby would not drag Deirdre away the next day, but all too aware that his time was finite. Once Deirdre left Everdon Park, his chances of winning her would be slim.

He stood in the hall, finger tapping against the glossy oak banister, considering his predicament. Was his motive pity?

There was an element of compassion in his feelings. If Deirdre did not marry him, she might never marry at all. That would be a shame, but not a tragedy. She was a woman capable of living a full life without a husband. He knew, however, that she had qualities that would die if not tended, and that he was one of the few to see and cherish them. It did seem a pity that she go through life thinking herself unappealing to men.

He knew, too, that he was partly driven by convenience. He had little taste for starting a new search for a wife.

He imagined the scenario his mother had placed before him. How would he feel if he had to wave farewell to Deirdre, and woo elsewhere?

His hand tightened on the banister, driven by a surge of primitive possessiveness. Never. Bring another woman to be mistress here? See Deirdre, perhaps, wed to another man?

Never.

He loved Deirdre Stowe!

He took a moment to relish the full recognition, as he would relish the first taste of a magnificent Tokay wine, knowing that there was a pipe of it in his cellars.

Then he raced up the stairs two at a time and dashed to her door. He pulled himself to a halt, heart pounding, hands rather unsteady. This would not do. He was Don Juan. He could please any woman. Pray God, he could please the one who mattered.

He knocked. When there was no answer, he walked in.

Deirdre had been sitting miserably by the empty hearth. She turned, shocked that someone would invade her privacy. At the sight of Everdon, she felt the blood drain from her head.

"For God's sake, don't faint on me."

His harsh voice snapped back her wits a little. "Please go away, my lord. There is nothing to be said."

"Is there not, indeed? Why all this coldness? Of what am I accused? Do I not deserve to hear the charges?"

Deirdre rose to her feet, almost afraid of him in this mood. "I have no charges, my lord. It is just that everything is over."

"On the contrary. We are engaged to be married."

"A mere stratagem . . ."

"Nonsense. I told you earlier, Deirdre. I want to marry you."

"No!" She found she had retreated behind her chair as if she expected him to attack her.

"Why the devil not?"

"Stop *shouting* at me!"

They stood facing each other, breathing heavily with their anger.

She saw him take a deep breath. "I love you, Deirdre."

"Oh, very pretty, my lord. Am I to be twisted around your fingers by three easy words?"

"Easy! Damn it, Deirdre—"

"And stop swearing at me."

"Why the devil should I? You're enough to drive a man to drink. I love you. I love you. You are essential to my happiness. What else do you want to hear?"

"Good-bye?" Deirdre heard the cruel word escape her lips, and winced. But, oh, she wanted him to be gone. Surely without him in front of her, this pain would lessen: the pain of cutting free of a man she loved, but who did not love her.

"Why?" he asked quietly, all anger leashed.

His gentleness weakened her. Deirdre turned away. "I can't marry you, my lord, not least because you don't really want to marry me. You don't love me, though you are courteous enough to pretend. It's just that I'm quiet and won't be any trouble. And I'm here, which is easier than finding someone else . . ."

"Deirdre, for heaven's sake—"

"And I suppose that you were right. You proved that Howard didn't really love me, and so now you feel an obligation . . ." She made herself turn back. "I am grateful, truly I am. You saved me from a disaster, and now you're trying to mend my hurts. It is not necessary, though. I will mend well enough on my own."

"Will I?"

Deirdre shook her head. "Please stop trying to be noble, my lord. I know what I am, and I am not the sort of woman that men suffer for."

"You are a complete fool."

Deirdre flinched under his sharp tone, but she would not fall to brangling again. She went to her jewelry box and took out the diamond ring—the ring that she had only worn for a few brief hours. She held it out to him. "Please take this, my lord. I find we would not suit."

He took it thoughtfully. "It surely isn't so easy. What of your mother?"

"She will understand . . ." But Deirdre could not make it convincing. She wasn't sure what her mother would do.

"Will she? The suitor she does not favor has left. But the suitor she does favor is still committed."

"Oh, but surely . . ."

"But surely," he said. "If you truly wish to be free of this engagement, Lady Deirdre, I think we will have to go through with our original plan."

"You will arrange to be found with a woman?"

The thought of catching Everdon entangled with another woman, even a maid, made Deirdre almost sick with misery. But it would serve to free him of his obligation, as well as to allow her to go home. She nodded bravely. "Very well. What must I do?"

"I will put it all in hand. Just come where and when I summon you. Promise? I don't want to go through this for nothing." There was even some humor in his tone.

"I promise."

"Just remember, Deirdre. I am doing this for you."

She felt like Joan of Arc on the pyre. "I will not blame you in my heart, my lord."

"I'll hold you to that."

With that he left, and she could be miserable in

peace. How right she had been. Just a little token protest and he had agreed to set her free. Don Juan clearly felt nothing particular for her, and soon would be delightfully happy with a pretty bride.

" 'If it were done when 'tis done, then 'twere well it were done quickly.' " Everdon found himself muttering the line from Macbeth and really began to fear for his sanity. What was he supposed to do with a little fool who wouldn't believe she was loved? Couldn't believe she was desired.

Within a few hours her brothers would be home. He felt no surety that she wouldn't persuade her mother to leave on the morrow. Once out of sight, she could be snapped up by some other man.

Had she forgotten that kiss they had shared? How could she discount that passion?

Clearly she could, so he must try some other measures. Risky ones.

Everdon gave some careful instructions to his staff: when they should keep out of sight, and when a couple of them should appear. Then he wrote three notes to be sent to the three ladies of the house.

That done, he went to the garden room. To set the scene, he stripped off his jacket, waistcoat, and cravat. On such a hot summer's day, it was a dashed good idea anyway.

He did not feel comfortable, though. He felt like a green lad engaged in his first assignation. What if she did not react as he expected? What if he had misjudged her feelings? Well, at least he would find out before they were committed beyond redemption.

When he sat on the sofa his restless fingers found a threadbare spot where the stuffing would soon work through. He looked around with new eyes. He hadn't realized quite how shabby some parts of his house had become. There was a damp stain above the glass doors and a hazardous hole in the faded carpet. His affairs had been in order for some years and it was clearly time he paid attention to his home. One of his wife's first duties, he decided, would be to help him refurbish his home.

One of Deirdre's first duties . . .

Deirdre crept tentatively in. Seeing him alone, she stopped, reddening with embarrassment. "Oh, I'm sorry . . . I must be too early . . ."

He stood, praying for all his skill. "No. I want to talk to you first."

"What about?"

He held out a hand and was much heartened when she trustingly placed hers in it. He thought perhaps it was going to be all right.

He drew her just a little closer. "When you are free, Deirdre, I am hoping you will look for a husband more to your taste. I think you will be better able to choose a husband if you know more about kissing. Now, while we are still betrothed, it wouldn't be entirely improper for me to show you."

"But we did . . ." She was deliciously pink and flustered, and he could feel the strain of keeping the situation light.

"Alas. I was upset. It was hardly my most skillful effort. Let me show you properly."

"Oh, I don't know . . ." But she did not retreat, and the longing in her eyes betrayed her.

He drew her into his arms, gently, slowly, giving her every chance to escape. "Please, *mi corazón*."

With a visible sigh of surrender, she nodded. "Very well, then."

He took a deep breath of relief and backed to the sofa to collapse there with her in his lap.

She balked a little at that. "My lord! Don! What of your . . . ? What if she . . . ?"

"She won't." He raised her small hands between them and kissed them with reverent care, concentrating on their pleasuring.

It was the kind of thing a woman liked, the kind of thing he'd done a hundred, a thousand times before, but now it was so hard. He did not want to use his skilled seducer's steps. He wanted to embrace her with all the passion of this morning, to kiss her, to lose himself in her forever ...

Deirdre looked down at his glossy hair, felt his lips tease her palms, and knew she was a fool. What pain she was creating here. The memories of this moment would be thorns in her heart forever, but she wanted them all the same.

How could kisses on the hand be so wonderful? Now his tongue was on her fingertips ...

"Oh my ..." She had whispered it aloud.

He looked up, and his dark eyes seemed darker and frighteningly intense. His arms encompassed her, and his lips wandered over her face—her cheeks, her chin, her temples, her eyelids—so that she felt she was drowning in kisses.

"Don ..." It was intended as a protest, but Deirdre could hear the longing in it.

Now his hand was wandering over her body. It was not bold enough to summon a protest, except that she thought perhaps she should protest. Except that she did not want to. At least he wasn't inside her clothing ...

"I thought you were to teach *me* to kiss," she managed to say.

"So I am, Deirdre. I have been demonstrating. Now, you kiss me."

She stared at him for a moment, then began to kiss his face as he had kissed hers. Oh, how she had wanted to do this; to pay homage to his lean cheeks, his perfect nose, his beautiful eyes ...

He slid back so she was on top of him. His shirt stood open at the neck, so she kissed his warm skin there. She was aware of his hands traveling over her back. Through her fine muslin it almost felt as if they touched her skin.

"Bite me," he said softly.

She looked up. "What?"

"Just little nips. It's another form of kissing. Like this." He captured her hand and took the fleshy part of her thumb in the gentle pressure of his teeth.

Deirdre sucked in a sharp breath. Then she surveyed him. "I feel like a diner choosing the most succulent piece of meat." Deirdre realized she was smiling at him. How could she be smiling at a time like this?

He grinned back. "I wait to be eaten."

She sank her teeth into his neck, but didn't think she hurt him. She relished the taste of his flesh, but when she released him she saw that she had made a dark mark there.

"Oh dear . . ."

"Marked me, have you? Fair's fair. You must let me mark you."

Deirdre swallowed, but nodded. A dim, distant part of her mind reminded her that she had come here for some other purpose, but nothing short of Armageddon could stop her from enjoying every last moment of this tryst.

He pushed her away slightly, surveying her as greedily as she had surveyed him. The very path of his eyes made her tremble.

He put out a hand and traced the low bodice of her dress, easing it down to uncover the upper swell of her breast. She captured his hand.

His eyes dared her. "Fair's fair, and you wouldn't want the mark where it could be seen, would you?"

With a mental apology to her mother, Deirdre released him, and his mouth wandered across her chest to settle on the spot he had marked, just an inch or two inside her neckline. She swayed back against his arm, and her own hands came to hold his head to her. He nuzzled lower and lower. His fingers brushed her thigh, and it felt as if he really was touching her bare skin . . .

"Good God!"

Her mother's voice shocked Deirdre back into her senses. She twisted her head to see her mother standing in the doorway, staring at her. Lucetta stood behind, looking amused. The butler and Joseph peered in from a distance.

Deirdre squeaked, and grabbed Everdon's head to pull him off her.

He was deliciously flushed and disordered, and for a moment she lost awareness that they had been caught.

"Lord Everdon," said Lady Harby awfully. "Remove your hand from my daughter!"

Deirdre looked down and found that his hand covered her right breast, but it was the only thing that did. She hastily tugged up her gown, and he eased his hand away as it became unnecessary.

"Oh, criminy . . ." Deirdre muttered. She would have leapt to her feet, but he was still all over her. She whispered frantically, "Get up, my lord!"

"Calm, light of my life. There is an art to this."

Deirdre realized that more than her bodice was disarranged. Most of her skirt was, too. His hand really *had* been on the naked skin of her thigh. Somehow—years of practice?—he pulled her to her feet and rearranged her clothing on one smooth movement, and turned them to face their accusers, keeping her safe in his arms.

"Well," said Lady Harby severely. "I've told you, Deirdre, let them inside your clothing and it's the altar for you. And we'd best not wait until September by the looks of it."

"We will certainly wait until September if Deirdre wishes to," said Everdon firmly. "There is no reason for haste."

"We'll at least have the betrothal in the papers immediately," countered her mother.

"Of course."

Deirdre looked between them and collected her wits. "Stop! I am not marrying Lord Everdon."

"You most certainly are, miss, after a scene like that. Look at the pair of you!"

"He tricked me!"

"Tricked you? How, pray?"

Deirdre turned to Everdon for support, then the truth dawned. Rage bloomed, and she swung back and clouted him with all the strength in her arm. She cried out at the pain in her hand, but she had the satisfaction of seeing him knocked backward. Of course, he would not have fallen if his heel had not caught in a hole in the threadbare carpet, but there was great satisfaction in seeing him tumble to the floor.

She stood over him, arms akimbo. "I told you I'd hit you."

He lay there laughing. "I knew you were a woman of your word. Marry me, Deirdre. Please?"

"Why?" It was almost a wail.

"I haven't finished the kissing lessons."

She hurled a musty cushion at him. She looked for further ammunition and threw his jacket over his face.

He pushed out from under it. "Is that a hint that you want me to dress, dear heart?"

"That's a hint that I want you to stop making fun of me!"

He leapt lightly to his feet, but there was nothing light about his expression. "I truly want you to marry me, Deirdre. You have every quality that I wish for in a wife, but in addition, I adore you. Think back over the last fifteen minutes or so. That was not a mild, convenient passion, Deirdre. That was deep desire. I desire you, body and soul."

Deirdre looked anxiously at the watchers, for

though Everdon seemed unaware of them, she was. She saw that the servants, at least, had gone. "Why on earth did you stage this farce?"

"To show you what we have here. You could have stopped me at any time, but you wanted that as much as I. But also to compromise you. This time, one way or another, I will keep you with me."

"You are trying to trap me!"

"Yes. But what am I to do? I can make you happy, *cara* . . ." Then he spread his hands and sighed. "I fool myself. I cannot hold you like this. Even in your own interests I cannot use the whip. No one here will speak of what they have seen, Deirdre—I promise you that. You are free. If your heart is free."

Deirdre sucked in a breath. This final gesture, the act of setting her free, was the one that broke the chains. "You truly do love me," she whispered in wonder.

"To distraction. As I have never loved before."

"But why? I am not pretty."

"If I were to be scarred tomorrow, would you cease to love me?"

"No,, but—" She glared at him. "I have not said I love you, sir."

"Do you not? If you don't, I will find a way to make you love me as I love you."

Deirdre was overwhelmed that he would say these things before others. "I don't know . . . *Why* do you love me?"

He reached out and touched her cheek. "Why do you love me? I love you for your courage, and your honor. For the way you dance, and the way you smile. I love the child that is still in you, and the woman you are beginning to be. I love you as you are. What more can I say?"

There was almost a plea in that, and Deirdre answered it by going into his arms. "This frightens me a little."

He held her close. "It terrifies me," he admitted with a laugh. "But to be without you would terrify me more."

Deirdre had to ask. "And your first wife? Is she still in your heart?"

"Oh, love, my heart and she parted long ago. I wept for the person she might have been, in another time and another place, and for the misery of her passing. There is no one but you."

Deirdre had no choice but to believe. He produced the diamond ring with a question in his eyes. Blushing, she extended her hand and let him slip it once more onto her finger.

At that moment Rip and Henry burst in. "Where is everybody?" Harry demanded. "What a day. What a fight!"

"Yes, wasn't it?" murmured Everdon.

"Thought it'd go on forever!" declared Rip. "Wasn't sure of the outcome at all."

"Neither was I," mouthed Everdon, and Deirdre bit her lip against a grin.

"Until the victor landed that blow," said Henry. "What a right!"

Sent him crashing to the floor!" said Rip. "Wouldn't have missed it for the world."

Everdon turned Deirdre in his arms, and stood with his chin resting on her head. "My sentiments entirely, Lord Ripon."

"What?" said Rip. "You weren't there, were you, Everdon? Corking contest, wasn't it? Touch and go. Some clever maneuvering, but plenty of close work. They really went at it toward the end."

Deirdre could feel Don Juan shaking with the laughter she was fighting down. She elbowed him, and he kissed her cheek.

Rip looked around. "Why's everyone in here, anyway? Not to be discourteous or anything, Everdon, but this room ain't your best spot. Could do with a bit of refurbishing. There's a hole in the carpet there that could cause an accident."

"How true. Deirdre will doubtless see to it."

"Not at all," said Deirdre sweetly. "I shall preserve it as a valued memento."

Rip stared at them in bemusement, then his gaze became fixed on Everdon's neck. "I say . . ."

Lady Harby interrupted. "It lacks but fifteen minutes to dinnertime, Ripon, and you are in all your dirt. Get along with you. And you, too, Henry." She turned to leave with Lucetta, but turned back. "And you, too, Everdon. And I'll thank you to behave yourself until September!"

They were alone again. Everdon turned Deirdre gently in his arms and they collapsed together in helpless laughter.

When she recovered Deirdre gasped, "I don't feel at all like myself."

He hugged her. "I don't feel like Don Juan, either. Will you mind being boringly domestic, and attending to my rather tattered home?"

She smiled up at him. "I can think of nothing I'd like more, Don. Except, perhaps," she added with a sliding look, "another kissing lesson?"

His eyes darkened, but he pushed her away. "Oh no, sweet temptress. That will have to wait until September."

Author's Note

❧❦❧

1814 was the year of the false peace.

England had been at war for nearly twenty years, and when the Emperor Napoleon abdicated, the people were ecstatic to think that it was finally over and that the "Corsican Monster" was safe on the island of Elba.

It was a year of great social excitement. In April Louis XVIII returned in triumph to Paris. France had been closed to the English for nearly a generation, but prior to that, Paris had been the cultural center of Europe, a place of almost mystical attractions. Now that France was open to them again, a good portion of the English aristocracy accompanied Louis.

By June, the *haut ton* had swarmed back to London, for the Allied Sovereigns—Tsar Alexander and King Frederick-William of Prussia—were to make a state visit.

There were receptions, balls, and dinners of unparalleled magnificence, and at last the waltz was danced at Almack's. The waltz had been danced in England, but had not been considered quite proper. When Tsar Alexander decided to dance it at Almack's, however, the matter was settled once and for all.

It was not only the cream of society who wanted to celebrate. So did the ordinary folk, and they gathered in London in unprecedented numbers to take part in the festivities. Their particular favorite was not the monarchs, but the Prussian general, Blucher, who had played such a large part in defeating Napoleon. His carriage was almost invariably pulled through the streets, not by horses, but by willing members of the populace.

On Sunday, June 11, the tsar and the king of Prussia rode in Hyde Park, and it was estimated that over 150,000 people were there to watch. On the twentieth, there was a review by the monarchs of 10,000 troops. The unfortunate result was that parts of the park were little more than trampled mud. Matters became worse, because after the Allied Sovereigns had left, the main London parks were the scene of festivities put on expressly for the people. A wonderful time was had, but it took years for the parks to recover.

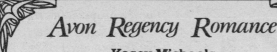

Avon Regency Romance

Kasey Michaels

THE CHAOTIC MISS CRISPINO
76300-1/$3.99 US/$4.99 Can

THE DUBIOUS MISS DALRYMPLE
89908-6/$2.95 US/$3.50 Can

THE HAUNTED MISS HAMPSHIRE
76301-X/$3.99 US/$4.99 Can

Loretta Chase

THE ENGLISH WITCH 70660-1/$2.95 US/$3.50 Can
ISABELLA 70597-4/$2.95 US/$3.95 Can
KNAVES' WAGER 71363-2/$3.95 US/$4.95 Can
THE SANDALWOOD PRINCESS
71455-8/$3.99 US/$4.99 Can

THE VISCOUNT VAGABOND
70836-1/$2.95 US/$3.50 Can

Jo Beverley

EMILY AND THE DARK ANGEL
71555-4/$3.99 US/$4.99 Can

THE FORTUNE HUNTER
71771-9/$3.99 US/$4.99 Can

THE STANFORTH SECRETS
71438-8/$3.99 US/$4.99 Can

Buy these books at your local bookstore or use this coupon for ordering:

Mail to: Avon Books, Dept BP, Box 767, Rte 2, Dresden, TN 38225   C
Please send me the book(s) I have checked above.
❏ My check or money order— no cash or CODs please— for $_____is enclosed
(please add $1.50 to cover postage and handling for each book ordered— Canadian residents
add 7% GST).
❏ Charge my VISA/MC Acct#_____Exp Date_____
Minimum credit card order is two books or $6.00 (please add postage and handling charge of
$1.50 per book — Canadian residents add 7% GST). For faster service, call
1-800-762-0779. Residents of Tennessee, please call 1-800-633-1607. Prices and numbers
are subject to change without notice. Please allow six to eight weeks for delivery.

Name_____
Address_____
City_____State/Zip_____
Telephone No._____

REG 0693

*If you enjoyed this book,
take advantage
of this special offer.
Subscribe now and get a*

FREE
Historical
Romance

No Obligation (a $4.50 value)

Each month the editors of True Value select the four *very best* novels
from America's leading publishers of romantic fiction. Preview them
in your home *Free* for 10 days. With the first four books you receive,
we'll send you a FREE book as our introductory gift. No Obligation!

If for any reason you decide not to keep them, just return them
and owe nothing. If you like them as much as we think you will, you'll
pay just $4.00 each and save at *least* $.50 each off the cover price.
(Your savings are *guaranteed* to be at least $2.00 each month.) There
is NO postage and handling – or other hidden charges. There are no
minimum number of books to buy and you may cancel at any time.

**Send in
the Coupon
Below**

To get your FREE historical romance fill out the
coupon below and mail it today. As soon as we
receive it we'll send you your FREE Book along
with your first month's selections.

- -

**Mail To: True Value Home Subscription Services, Inc., P.O. Box 5235
120 Brighton Road, Clifton, New Jersey 07015-5235**

YES! I want to start previewing the very best historical romances being published today. Send
me my FREE book along with the first month's selections. I understand that I may look them
over FREE for 10 days. If I'm not absolutely delighted I may return them and owe nothing.
Otherwise I will pay the low price of just $4.00 each: a total $16.00 (at least an $18.00 value)
and save at least $2.00. Then each month I will receive four brand new novels to preview as
soon as they are published for the same low price. I can always return a shipment and I may
cancel this subscription at any time with no obligation to buy even a single book. In any event
the FREE book is mine to keep regardless.

Name		
Street Address		Apt. No.
City	State	Zip
Telephone		
Signature		

Terms and prices subject to change. Orders subject
(if under 18 parent or guardian must sign)   to acceptance by True Value Home Subscription
Services, Inc.

77281-7